JOCK AND JILL

A CHARLOTTE ZOLOTOW BOOK

A novel by

Robert Lipsyte

Harper & Row, Publishers

Library of Congress Cataloging in Publication Data
Lipsyte, Robert.
    Jock and Jill.

    Summary: Jack Ryder, aspiring baseball star, meets
Jillian, a girl who makes him reevaluate all his pri-
orities.
    [1. Baseball—Fiction]   I. Title.
PZ7.L67Jo   [Fic]   81-47723
ISBN 0-06-023899-2   AACR2
ISBN 0-06-023900-X (lib. bdg.)

For Ruby

JOCK AND JILL

1

He was walking out to the pitcher's mound for the bottom of the ninth inning when he first saw her. She was perched on the rail of the metal fence behind the home team bench, shooting pictures. The camera hid her face, but he could tell from the rest of her that she wasn't his type at all. Too tall, too busty, too dark. An avalanche of frizzy black hair tumbled over her shoulders. He didn't even like what she was wearing, a purple jump suit. But something inside him stirred at the sight of her.

He clamped a lid on it. Get tough, Jack, he told himself. Three more outs and we win. Next stop, Yankee Stadium.

The girl shifted position on the rail. She lowered her camera and studied him. Her eyes were large and dark.

He looked away. Think ball, Jack.

The afternoon sun was a pale yellow in the gray Bronx sky. It was hot for late June. He took a deep breath. Mistake. The air stank of chemicals and car fumes.

He threw his warm-up pitches. His arm felt heavier, thicker. It was no longer the bullwhip he had cracked through eight masterful innings. Even the sound of the ball hitting the catcher's mitt seemed softer. His one-run lead suddenly seemed very shaky.

Coach Burg walked out to the mound. "Elbow hurts, doesn't it?"

As if in answer, the dull, steady ache in Jack's elbow began to narrow and sharpen. There was a buzzing sensation. The painkiller was wearing off.

Jack shrugged "It'll be okay."

"You know it, big fella." Coach Burg looked him in the eye. "Think about this when you hurt. Three more outs and we're in Yankee Stadium. No team from New Jersey ever made the Metro Area final before. Be college coaches and pro scouts all over the place."

Coach Burg turned his back and sauntered off the field. The umpire called, "Play ball!" The first Bronx Vocational High School batter stepped into the box.

The catcher, Pete Reynolds, began signaling pitches, but Jack shook him off. He'd call his own game, throw what the elbow would let him throw. Behind him, Joey DiNola, the shortstop, was leading the infield in chatter to keep them alert.

"Hey, Jack-eeeeee."

Donnie's shrill voice cut through the chatter and the

4

neighborhood noises of trucks grinding past and transistor radios blasting Latin music. He imagined Donnie bouncing up and down in his seat behind third base. Beside him, Grandma would be scanning the field with her quick, pecking eyes, missing nothing. Dad would be wincing and grunting with every pitch, and Mom would be glancing back and forth from Jack to Dad, afraid Jack might get hurt or Dad might bust an artery cheering for him. And Kristie, beautiful, perfect Kristie, her bright blue eyes fastened on Jack, would be fingering the tiny gold tennis racket charm hooked to her gold chain. Jack had given it to her last month for her seventeenth birthday.

Can't let them down, he thought. Got to stay up. Tough. Hard. He aimed his mind like a laser beam at the batter sixty feet six inches away. Got him on a fastball last time, he'll be looking for it again. Fool him with a change-up.

He struck out the first batter.

Dad's voice boomed, "Way to go, Jumpin' Jack. Hold 'em, Nearmont Tigers, two more outs."

The pain in his elbow was more persistent now, the buzzing a tiny chain saw biting into tendon and bone. Once the painkilling injection wore off entirely, the elbow would be on fire. Every pitch would be an explosion of agony. He knew he could guts out the pain, he had done that before, but there was nothing he could do about the inflamed tendons causing it. Once the involuntary spasms began, his curveball would hang and his fastball would lose its jump.

5

The second batter dug in. Jack threw him two balls and felt an electric current burn through his arm. He tried to sneak a three-quarter speed fastball over the plate, but the batter smashed it deep into center field, the longest drive off Jack the entire game. Bucky Flynn caught it on the run, one-handed. Two out.

The third batter slammed a triple.

Coach Burg walked slowly out to the mound to give Jack a chance to rest. You'd better hurry, thought Jack, before I can't raise my arm high enough to pick my nose.

He looked around to keep his mind off his arm. The girl in the purple jump suit was aiming her camera at half a dozen Puerto Ricans who were sitting in the stands cheering the Bronx team. She tossed her head to clear away hair from the front of her lens. Something about the way the black strands settled on her firm, rounded arm spread warmth through Jack's stomach.

Not your type, Jack. He turned toward third base and brushed the peak of his cap with the thumb of his glove, the secret sign to Kristie that he was thinking of her. Kristie blew him a kiss.

Coach Burg finally reached the mound. He was sweating. "This is it, Jack. I can bring in Kazuto or Josh, but if you can go the distance you'll have something to be proud of the rest of your life. This is where you find out if you're a man."

"I can do it." Jack's heart fluttered.

"Everybody's counting on you. One more out." Coach Burg turned and trudged off the field.

6

Jack waited until his breathing was rhythmical again, fast and shallow but regular, before he stepped on the rubber. His first pitch was low, in the dirt. Pete barely scooped it up. If it had gone past him, the run would have scored. Tie game. No way this arm can last into extra innings, thought Jack. Got to end it now. Everything I've got.

The infield chattered like ducks on the reservoir back home, and Dad and Donnie clapped and chanted and Coach Burg shouted and the Puerto Ricans behind the Bronx bench hooted and cursed him. He checked the runner on third and pitched.

The batter swung. The ball shot straight up into the oozing sun between home plate and first base.

Instinctively, Jack moved with the crack of the bat. He had a better angle than Pete. Todd Newman, the first baseman, had bad legs and was slow.

Jack lunged off the mound toward the white line. The ball reappeared, a nimbus of light plummeting foul behind the Bronx bench. He sprinted across foul territory. The Bronx players scattered out of his way as he leaped onto their bench and hurled himself over the top of the fence.

He was flying, arms outstretched. He saw only the ball. A purple cotton wall loomed in front of him. A black metal cylinder appeared in the corner of his left eye. He plunged into the purple cotton wall. Soft. The cylinder smashed into his left eye. The ball fell into his glove.

2

"Consider yourself lucky," said Jack's father, at breakfast.

"If you were lucky," said his grandmother, "you wouldn't have gotten poked in the eye in the first place."

Jack kept his good eye aimed at his plate and his swollen, watery left eye closed against the bright sunlight filling the kitchen. Carefully, he mopped up the last orange streaks of his fried eggs with a scrap of wholewheat muffin. They're at it again, he thought.

"You're gonna bounce back stronger, Jackie," said Dad. "A great athlete discovers himself coming off an injury."

"I thought Jack discovered himself last year," said Grandma sarcastically, "when he broke his leg."

"I'm so glad he's not playing football anymore," said Mom. "I always worried."

"Don't kid yourself, Jean," said Grandma, "the pressure's worse now, they've got the boy thinking baseball twenty-four hours a day twelve months a year."

"Jack can handle the pressure," said Dad.

"That's not the message his elbow is sending out," said Grandma. "It was bothering you yesterday, wasn't it?"

Before Jack could answer, his father guffawed. "Message? I always thought the elbow was a joint, not an answering service."

Grandma ignored him. "When you're under great pressure, Jack, the most vulnerable part of your mind or body is always the first to be affected."

"Pressure? We're talking about a seventeen-year-old superathlete in peak condition who happens to have a slightly strained tendon. Which is being treated, thank you."

"The symptoms are being treated," said Grandma. "With God knows what long-term side effects."

"How's the eye feel?" asked Mom, for the third time that morning.

For the third time, Jack replied, "Much better."

"You just take it easy today," said Mom. "Sit on the deck, get some sun."

The thought of nothing to do, no game or workout to disappear into, tensed the muscles of his shoulders and neck. "Maybe I'll take Donnie fishing," he said.

"Awwwwwww-riiiiight," shouted Donnie, spilling milk. His moon face beamed. That settles today, thought Jack.

The phone rang. His mother jumped to answer it.

"Got to start thinking about the game at the Stadium," said Dad.

"Can't you let the boy rest?" asked Grandma.

"He's got all summer to rest."

"Jack?" Mom pressed the phone receiver against her chest. "It's for you. That girl from yesterday."

"What does she want?"

"To talk to you. Here." She held out the receiver.

He felt suddenly uneasy. "Tell her I'm not home."

Mom covered the receiver again. "I've already told her you're right here. She sounds very nice. She's concerned about your eye."

"As she should be," said Grandma.

"Talk to her," urged Dad. "What's it going to cost you?"

"I don't want to talk to her."

Mom looked puzzled. "Why not?"

He didn't know why. He said, "I just don't feel like it, okay?"

Mom turned her back on them and spoke into the phone. "He's not feeling well right now. Could you call back later? Fine." She wrote a name and a telephone number with a New York City area code on the memo board beside the phone. "Yes, I will. And thank you so much for calling." She hung up and turned sharply

10

on Jack. "That was very discourteous. Not like you at all. She sounded upset."

"Why go out of your way to antagonize anyone?" asked Dad.

"Maybe you should thank her," said Grandma. "Give her a shot at the other eye."

"It was an accident," said Mom.

Jack stood up. "I'm going upstairs, stretch out for a little while."

"Your eye?" asked Mom.

"Just a little headache," he admitted. He never liked to use injury or pain or fatigue as an excuse, but sometimes it was the only way he could get away from them all.

"What about fishing?" Donnie's lower lip trembled.

"When your cartoons are over, come up and get me."

As he climbed the carpeted steps to his bedroom, his elbow began to throb in rhythm with his head. In all the excitement over his eye, he had forgotten about the elbow until Grandma had brought it up. After the accident, there had been a careening ride in a police car with its siren wailing. Then X rays at the hospital emergency room. An examination by an ophthalmologist. After all that, only a butterfly bandage under his eyebrow and a black eye. No damage to the eye. The cut from the rim of the girl's camera lens hadn't even required stitches.

Jack eased himself onto his bed and slipped a cassette of country and western hits into the tape deck. Willie

11

and Waylon usually relaxed him, loosened his neck and shoulder muscles when they clenched with tension.

But the music wasn't working this morning, it wasn't massaging his body and soothing his mind. He thought about the girl in the purple jump suit. What was so special about her? He hardly ever noticed girls while he was pitching, and when he did, he put them right out of his mind again. And why had he been afraid to talk to her? He turned to bury his face in his pillow and blot out the girl's image. Pain clawed at his elbow.

It'll hurt tonight, he thought. Can't hardly bend it, much less hold Kristie. Have to move very carefully. Of all nights. Her parents won't be home till very late and we'll have her house all to ourselves.

Just as soon skip doing it tonight. Don't feel in the mood. Skip Eric's party, too. Bunch of loudmouths.

The thought surprised him. Why so down, Jack? Just won the Metro Area semifinal, going to pitch in Yankee Stadium in four days. How many guys just finished their junior year in high school get to pitch in the Stadium?

Donnie's heavy footsteps on the stairs were a relief.

Jack sat up and forced a smile. Got to be cheerful for Donnie. He's so sensitive.

Donnie knocked.

"Sorry," yelled Jack, "only Donnie can come in."

"Heeeeeere's Donnie." The door swung open and Donnie burst in, all 175 pounds of him. There's a project for this summer, thought Jack, trim off some of his winter flab.

"Ready to catch some fish?"

12

"Big ones." Donnie stretched out his arms.

Mom slipped into the room right behind him. "You sure you're up to it, Jack? Donnie can come shopping with Grandma and me."

Donnie's face fell.

"No, I'm looking forward to it."

Donnie grinned and clapped.

He could tell Mom had more to say. Might as well get it over with now. She never pressed too hard, anyway.

"Donnie, go get the can for the worms. Wait for me on the deck."

"How long?"

"Four minutes. Check it on your watch."

"Okay." Donnie lumbered out.

Softly, Mom asked, "Is everything all right?"

"I'm fine. You heard what the doctor said."

"I mean"—she bit her lip—"is *everything* all right? Is anything else bothering you?"

"Like what?" He was so used to playing dumb It came naturally now, he thought.

"Like anything," she said gently. "Oh, Jackie, sometimes I wish you'd talk a little more freely, say what you're thinking."

"I'm not thinking anything special."

"Well. If you ever want to tell me anything, you know you can." She bent forward suddenly and kissed his cheek. "Hamburgers tonight? Outside?"

"Sounds good."

She backed toward the door, smiling. "Don't forget

to call that girl. Her number's on the board. And Kristie called. She figured you wouldn't want to drive tonight, so she'll pick you up at eight-thirty. Wasn't that thoughtful?"

"Yeah."

When she was gone, he sank into the pillow. Maybe catch a few z's. Then he thought of Donnie, sitting on the deck, his lips moving with the blinking numbers on his watch.

Slowly, carefully, he eased himself off the bed.

3

"Do fish cry?" asked Donnie.

"I don't think so," said Jack.

"Even when you hook them?"

"I don't think fish have feelings like you and I do."

"Oh." That satisfied Donnie. He leaned against a tree and concentrated on holding his rod very still. He didn't have the coordination to cast his line, but he made up for that with an incredible patience. He could sit and stare at his red-and-white bobber for hours.

Jack stretched out alongside him. The sun on his bare chest and legs felt kind and healing. The ache in his elbow was distant.

The reservoir sparkled. It was his favorite place in Nearmont, in the entire county. He tried to remember the last time he had just fallen out in the sun. Last year, when the All-County team was invited down to Atlantic City to play a round-robin tournament, he had gotten up early one morning and stretched out by the pool of the motel. One of the coaches had chased him back to his room. He didn't want Jack getting dehydrated and sunburned.

"Is it sissy to cry?" asked Donnie.

"Not if you've got a good reason."

"Did you cry when you got poked in the eye?"

"No."

"I did. I was really scared when you fell down. I thought you were dead."

"It was one of those things that looked worse than it was," said Jack. "Don't think about it."

Jack dozed. Got to do this more. Just fall out with Donnie. He felt his body melt and leak away. Good for both of us. Get away from all the hassle.

It seemed like only a minute later that he was sitting up shivering. The sun was low. Donnie was in the same position, studying his bobber.

"Let's go. Dinnertime."

"I didn't catch anything."

"We'll come again soon." Jack stood up slowly. Every muscle complained.

"Promise?" Donnie clambered to his feet. His soft stomach and thighs wobbled.

"We've got to start building up those muscles."

"What do you call this?" Donnie flexed a bicep.

"World's largest marshmallow." He pushed Donnie up the embankment.

Donnie reached the dirt road and panted. He's really out of shape, thought Jack. Maybe we could start jogging together before breakfast. After the Stadium game.

"You want to hear a secret?" asked Donnie.

"Sure."

"I didn't use a hook."

"How'd you expect to catch a fish?"

"I didn't want to catch a fish." Donnie's lip trembled. "You mad?"

"I don't care. Why do you go fishing if you don't want to catch a fish?"

"To be with you."

Jack laughed and threw his left arm around Donnie's neck. Donnie hugged him. Jack tickled him until Donnie was giggling wildly and begging him to stop.

They ambled toward home, arms around each other, on shady streets without sidewalks. A mild breeze carried the smells of backyard cookouts. Kids playing Frisbee and men tending their lawns waved and called to Jack. He felt good, dopey from the sun, warmed by Donnie's happiness. He was hungry, and he imagined the thick, juicy hamburgers sizzling on the barbecue. A few beers and some laughs at Eric's party. His ribs didn't hurt so much now; so long as he and Kristie took it easy . . .

"Who's that?" asked Donnie.

A long black limousine was parked in their driveway.

A chauffeur dozed at the wheel. The limo bore official New York City license plates.

"I don't know," he said, but he suddenly felt keyed up, on edge. He knew. He didn't know how he knew, but he did. It was her.

4

His father said, "Jill came all the way out from the city to . . ."

"Jillian," she corrected politely, but firmly. She was marching across the deck toward Jack, her hand outstretched. She was wearing a purple sun dress with white polka dots.

"You don't like to be called Jill?" asked Mom.

"No. Jill sounds like someone who followed somebody else up a hill." She turned back to Jack. "I didn't think you'd ever call me back, and I wanted you to know I'm really sorry about your eye."

He shook her hand. It was strong and warm. She was even taller than he had thought. The mass of frizzy black hair swirled around large, bold features.

"You came all the way out just to apologize?"

19

"I hit you in the eye, didn't I? I'm really glad you're okay."

"Would you like to eat with us?" asked Mom. "There's plenty, and we were just going to sit down now that the boys are back."

Jillian glanced at the hamburgers on the gas barbecue and the bowls of salad and potato chips on the redwood picnic table. "Thanks, but I'm not eating meat this summer. I'm trying to clean my head."

"Something to drink?" asked Dad. "We've got lemonade and soda and . . ."

"How do you clean your head?" asked Donnie.

Jack tensed as Jillian turned to stare at Donnie, who had come up the deck steps behind him. A lot of people had trouble at first, dealing with a big, handsome fifteen-year-old with the mind of a little kid.

Jillian smiled. "That's just an expression I use. It means my mind is full of thoughts that make me feel bad. I think red meat gives me bad thoughts, and fresh vegetables and grains clean them out. Hi, I'm Jillian."

"I'm Donnie." He raised his hand very slowly. He wasn't used to shaking hands. He grinned as Jillian pumped his limp arm.

Jack exhaled. She had handled that really well. He asked, "Is that your limo outside?"

"It's the Mayor's," she said. "He let me borrow it because he's afraid you might sue the city if we aren't nice to you."

"You know the Mayor personally?" asked Dad.

"He's a real close friend of my parents. He's been like an uncle to me."

"Well," said Dad, impressed. He raised his beer can in a toast. "To his reelection."

"He's going to have a hard campaign," said Jillian. She dropped into a redwood armchair. "A lot of people in the city don't appreciate the job he's done."

"I do," said Dad. "On TV he comes across as a real tough customer. He's not soft on crime."

"And what do you think?" asked Grandma. She had been sitting quietly in the corner of the deck, studying Jillian.

"I'm still checking it out," said Jillian.

"And how does one do that?" asked Grandma in a tone that always made Jack think of the sharp, uneven little teeth of a ripsaw blade.

"I go around the city and talk to people."

"Just like that?" asked Mom. "You just go up to strangers and ask them questions?"

"I use my cameras to give me a reason for being somewhere, and then I get into conversations," said Jillian. Her large brown eyes sparkled as she talked, and her long hands punctuated her sentences. So confident, Jack thought, she seems so at ease in a new place.

She continued: "For example, at Jack's game yesterday, I met some people who invited me to a rally tomorrow in that little park across the street from Yankee Stadium."

Dad shuddered. "Watch yourself. It's worth your life

21

to walk around the South Bronx, even on a Sunday afternoon."

"Have you been there lately?" asked Jillian.

"Don't have to," said Dad. "You see that movie? Don't you watch TV?"

Jillian shook her head. "Hardly ever." She turned to Jack. "Do you?"

"Mostly for sports," said Jack.

"Are you going to play major league baseball?"

"He's had some feelers," said Dad proudly, "but we want him to get his education first. A number of big-time colleges are very interested."

"I thought you looked terrific," said Jillian. "You've got incredible kinetic flow."

"I bet you say that to all the boys," cracked Grandma.

Jillian laughed. She had a nice laugh, thought Jack, natural, from deep in her chest.

"I'm into kinetics these days." She looked directly at Donnie, who was frowning with confusion. "Kinetics is the study of movement, and baseball players are the best athletes to shoot. That's why I was at the game. Their movements are distinct and easy to follow, you can get clear shots, they aren't all jumbled up like soccer and football and basketball players."

She really seemed to enjoy center court, thought Jack. He didn't think she was that much older than he was, eighteen or nineteen at the most, but there was something about her, experience, maybe, or sophistication, that made her seem very different from anyone he knew. He had an urge to reach out and touch her face. Her

22

skin was pale, in sharp contrast to her black hair. It looked very soft.

"I hope you'll send us some of your pictures," said Mom. "I'd love a good picture of Jack."

"I'll make you up a batch of extra prints," said Jillian.

"You've got your own darkroom?" asked Jack.

"The commune has one."

"Commune?" Grandma perked up. "I thought all the hippies were gone."

"Oh, we're not hippies," laughed Jillian. "This is a community of young people who are working through their energy blocks."

Dad contemplated his beer can and Mom smiled blankly. Donnie was lost. Grandma caught Jack's eye and winked. He could tell she was cranking up. She hadn't spent forty years as a school secretary without having something to say about almost everything.

"Energy blocks?" asked Grandma.

"Right." Jillian drew a square in the air with her forefingers. "Energy blocks keep you from achieving your potential. They're obstacles. They stop the flow. We're working through them."

"And exactly how do you do that?" asked Grandma.

"Each of us does it in his or her own special way," said Jillian. "Some with music or painting or dance or creative writing. I do it with photography."

"Do what?" persisted Grandma.

Jillian began to fidget in her chair. "We're trying to get to a place. From somewhere else."

It was quiet on the deck. Mom and Dad glanced at

23

each other. Donnie sat very still, sensing something wrong.

"And where is that?" ripsawed Grandma.

"Where is what?" Jillian fished a little silver box out of a pocket in her sundress and opened it. Her voice had lost its confidence.

Jack felt an overwhelming urge to rescue her, to snatch her away from Grandma's cutting edge, but before he could say anything, Grandma asked, "Where is somewhere else?"

Jillian took a white capsule out of the box and swallowed it. "It's hard to explain," she said weakly.

Jack said, "It was really nice, your coming all the way out here."

Jillian smiled gratefully. "You've really been so understanding. I should have gotten my camera out of your way, but I was so busy shooting, I didn't realize how close you were."

"Well, I'm okay and we won. No problem."

She looked at her watch and stood up. "I'd better get the car back. It was nice meeting all of you."

She shook hands all around. Jack followed her down the steps and out to the limo. The driver jerked awake as Jack opened the back door.

He tried to think of something smooth to say, but the best he could come up with was, "Take it easy. See you around." It sounded dumb to him even as he was saying it.

But she smiled and said, "I hope I'll see you again." She sounded as if she meant it.

He watched the limo back out of the driveway. She waved through the rear window. Neighbors gawked as the limo glided down the street and out of sight.

When he got back to the deck, Dad and Grandma were at it again.

"You didn't have to put her on the spot like that," said Dad. "She was a guest here."

"She invited herself," said Grandma.

"I thought she made a real effort to be sociable," said Mom.

"She could be a helluva contact for Jackie," said Dad. "She could get the Mayor to write him a recommendation for college next year."

"He probably won't even be mayor next year," said Grandma. "What did you think of her, Jack?"

He shrugged. "She was all right."

"I know that type," said Grandma. "Rich and spoiled and crazy. Maybe we ought to sue the city."

5

Kristie was unusually quiet on the ride to the party. She hunched over the wheel, her blue eyes squinty, and murmured, "Sorry," every time the car jounced over a pothole. She rarely drove when they were together, and her perfect features were scrunched up with the strain of giving him a smooth, painless ride. He knew he should tell her to relax, that he wasn't feeling particularly fragile. But he also didn't feel much like getting into a conversation. He was thinking of Jillian. He wondered if boys lived at the commune. He felt a splinter of jealousy. Then he felt stupid. What do I care? Don't even know the girl. Rich and spoiled and crazy.

As soon as they walked into Eric Cowan's house, Jack was sorry they had come. Eric sang out, "Here they are, Mister and Mizz A-mer-i-ca," and people crowded around to congratulate him on yesterday's game and ask about his eye. Jack replayed the last inning at least three times before someone pressed a cold can of beer into his hand. Kristie disappeared from his side. He wasn't sure exactly when because he didn't miss her right away.

He finished a second can and started to look for Kristie, but Gary Boda pulled him into a corner. He had never liked Gary much, even though Gary had caught his first high school no-hitter, two seasons ago. Gary had just finished his freshman year at Wicklin State, and he held Jack's arms as he raved about the athletic dorms.

"You gotta check it out," said Gary, in a hoarse whisper. "Jack-o, there is nothing low-rent about baseball at State. We get everything football and basketball gets, plus a spring training trip to Florida. Can you get your arms around that, huh?"

Jack nodded and tried to move around Gary, but his grip tightened. "Listen, promise you won't sign a letter of intent with any other college till you check out State."

"I don't have to make a decision till next year."

"They're gonna be on you like crabs, especially if you're semi-great at the Stadium Wednesday."

"Coach Burg's been handling all the recruiters, him and my father."

"I hear old Burgie gets a bonus for every blue-chipper he sends to Harrison, and they need pitching. They'd give Donnie a scholarship to get you." He stopped suddenly, realizing he had gone too far.

"Yeah." Jack pushed past Gary.

He spotted Kristie sitting in a corner of the patio, with Lisa Curry, who was crying. Todd Newman must be giving her a hard time again, he thought. Todd was getting to be a real juicer these days. It wasn't fun anymore to watch him tank up. Lisa always went crying to Kristie. Ever since he and Kristie became a regular couple in the spring of their sophomore year, people spilled out their troubles to them. To Kristie, anyway. He had made it clear after a while that he didn't like to ask advice or give it.

He backed away from the patio door before Kristie or Lisa saw him.

The party was getting louder, more crowded. He didn't recognize most of the new people coming in. Must be college friends of Eric's, he thought. Eric had just finished his sophomore year at Columbia. When Jack had been a freshman at Nearmont High, Eric had been a senior and his Varsity Big Brother. He'd been a good one, too, making sure none of the other players gave Jack a hard time and helping him get oriented to high school. Even after he'd graduated, Eric kept in touch; and when he had become head lifeguard at the Nearmont Swim Club this summer, the first two new guards he had hired were Jack and Kristie.

Jack got another beer from the tub of ice in the kitchen and wandered around. Eric's parents were spending the weekend at their place on the Jersey Shore. The way the party was revving up, it might still be going on when they came back. In the den, a bunch of guys he

knew from summer ball and a girl he had never seen
before were passing a joint and watching an X-rated
video cassette. One of the guys was announcing a play-
by-play of the sex scene in a bad imitation of Howard
Cosell. The announcer looked up at Jack.

"And here he is, folks, that peerless prodigy of the
pitching persuasion, Jumpin' Jack Ryder." The announcer waved him in. "Got some primo smoke here."

"No, thanks." Jack edged out.

He heard one of the other guys say, "There goes
the coach's dream, the perfect straight arrow."

The girl giggled. "Nobody's perfect."

Downstairs, flashing lights streaked the walls and ceiling of the family room with sudden slashes of shimmer-
ing color. The beer and the beat fogged his brain. He
tried to blink it clear. A big girl with an unruly bush
of black hair burst out of the pack of dancers and grabbed
his hand. He felt his heart flip over. *What's Jillian doing
here?*

He moved right into her. "How'd you get . . . Oh,
it's you, Kim."

"Who'd you think it was?"

"Sorry," he mumbled, "so hot in here . . ."

"You can dance with me. Look." Kim pointed toward
Kristie dancing with Brian Mills, head manager of the
baseball team.

"Later." He backed away, right into Todd.

"You gonna let that wimp come on to her like that?"

"Like what?" asked Jack.

"If you don't know, you're a wimp yourself," sneered

Todd. His words were slurred.

Eric stepped in between them. "Go get some air, Newman." He turned Todd and pushed him toward the garage door. He turned back to Jack and grabbed him in a bear hug. "Hey, little brother, how's it going?" Eric wasn't as tall as Jack, but he was big. Jack caught the force of Eric's hug on his elbows and grunted with pain. "What's the matter?"

"It's a little sore," said Jack.

"I got something for you." Eric led him up to his bedroom. A couple was making out on Eric's bed. They didn't seem to notice the intrusion.

"Percodan, dynamite stuff," said Eric, opening his top bureau drawer. He shook a pink pill out of a bottle. "I lived on these babies when I had my knee. Here you go."

Jack shook his head. "Thanks anyway."

"Why hurt if you don't have to? Besides, percs will make you feel gooooood, if you know what I mean."

"I'm in training."

"Who you kiddin'?" said Eric. "You let Doc May shoot all kinds of crap into your elbow."

"It's not the same thing," said Jack. "The shots are so I can pitch."

"Come off it, Jack. What's the difference if you're taking dope because they want you to or because you want to?"

"Nobody ever OD'ed from Doc May. Or burned out his brain with pot like Mickey Heller or cut her wrists like Kate Cogan or took too many . . ."

"Okay." Eric threw up his hands. "Jack Ryder never quits. Where's Kristie?"

"Downstairs."

"Everything cool with you guys?"

"Sure."

"Anything you want to tell me?"

"Nope."

Eric laughed and threw a slow punch at his jaw. "Anybody ever call you a motormouth?"

"Nope."

They both laughed and left the bedroom. The couple on the bed still didn't seem to notice.

In the hallway, Eric said, "What about the girl in the limo?"

"Where'd you hear about her?"

"You can't hide anything from your big brother."

"I got to take a leak," said Jack.

In the bathroom, he felt light-headed. Good thing I'm not driving home. He remembered that he hadn't mentioned Jillian's visit to Kristie. He had meant to, but he just hadn't gotten around to it.

He went back down to the living room. More new people were coming in. He found a wall to lean against. He was dizzy.

"Are you all right?" Kristie asked, touching his cheek. "You're flushed. And warm."

"I'm okay."

"Want to go now?" she asked.

"Do you?"

She nodded. She rose up on tiptoes to kiss him. He

had the impression she did it for the others. "Let's not waste that empty house," she said.

The ground swayed under him on the way out to Kristie's car. He felt better once he was sitting down. Kristie started the motor, then turned to him. "Who was she?"

"Who?"

"Jack, I hate it when you play dumb. You know who I mean. The girl in the limo."

"She was the one who hit me in the eye. She came out to apologize."

"She came all the way out from the city just to apologize?"

"She's a friend of the Mayor's. I guess he was afraid we'd sue the city or something."

That seemed to satisfy her. She pulled out of the driveway. "Why didn't you tell me about her?"

"It slipped my mind."

"How could something like that slip your mind? Do girls come out from the city in chauffered limousines every day, sit on your deck and . . ."

"If you know so much, why are you asking me?"

"It was all over the neighborhood. Amy Goodman called Lisa . . ."

"The Nearmont CIA."

"How do you think I felt tonight, everyone knew except me?"

"It wasn't such a big thing."

After a while, Kristie asked, "What was she like?"

"Nothing special. Sort of flaky." The instant it was

out of his mouth, he was sorry.

"Figures," said Kristie. "Lisa said she was one of those rich bitches who get off on jocks."

"How the hell would Lisa know?"

They fell silent. Just before they turned into Kristie's street, he switched on the radio and dialed the station that played country and western music.

"What are you doing?"

"I turned on the radio," he said.

"I can see that. I mean . . . *what are you doing?* You had nothing to say to me when I picked you up and you spent the party avoiding me and now . . ."

"Avoiding you? You were either whispering in a corner with Lisa Curry or coming on to Brian Mills."

"I don't believe this, Jack. I was pretending to enjoy myself so no one could tell I felt like a perfect fool."

"Nobody's perfect," said Jack.

"You're not taking this very seriously, are you?"

"Hey, Kris, lighten up."

"It's serious to me."

"It's boring to me."

"Oh." She steered into her driveway and cut the engine. The radio went off. "Bored, are you?"

"I just said this discussion is boring."

"You sure you're just not bored, period?"

He felt tired and dizzy. Maybe he was bored, period. Somehow, the prospect of going into her house and up to her bedroom didn't arouse him.

"Maybe you want me to drive you home," she said.

"Don't bother, I'll walk." The words surprised him

33

as much as they seemed to surprise her. They just fell out of his mouth. He heard her gasp as he opened the door and swung his legs out of the car.

He knew Kristie was too proud to call him. He never looked back.

6

Hundreds of men, women and children, Black and white and Hispanic, singing and waving signs, marched into the scrubby old neighborhood park across the street from Yankee Stadium.

Jack hung on the fence that enclosed the park and scanned the crowd for Jillian. It's hopeless, he thought. Never find her in this mob.

It had been a mistake to come here, a mistake to concoct lies for his parents and for Eric. He had told Mom and Dad that he was meeting a teammate who had tickets to the double-header at the Stadium. Then he had called Eric at the Swim Club to say he wouldn't be able to work today; the doctor had ordered him to stay out of the sun because of the antibiotics he was taking for the cut over his eye.

They had believed him. He had never made up complicated lies like these before. Never had to. He was sorry now. Thinking about the lies made him feel tense and chilly.

It was for nothing, a waste, all based on a flaky girl's offhand remark that she was going to a rally. She had probably changed her mind and gone to some fancy beach party on Long Island instead. It was a great beach day, a bright hot sun and a cooling breeze.

The marchers circled the inside of the park and surrounded a portable metal platform that had been erected in the middle of the field. Technicians swarmed over the platform, adjusting sound equipment.

Even if Jillian did show, and he found her, what would he say?

Fancy meeting you here.

Or, *Just happened to be in the South Bronx today, thought I'd drop in.*

Who wants to see her anyway? Not my type at all. One of those rich bitches who get off on jocks.

His feet, crotch, armpits and head were soaked with sweat. Usually, he'd go almost anywhere in a tank top, cutoffs and rubber shower clogs. The off-duty jock uniform, Kristie called it. But today he had dressed carefully in his hand-tooled brown western boots, his tightest white jeans and a plaid shirt rolled to the elbows and unbuttoned to the middle of his chest. He had tipped his beige Stetson low over his left eye to shield it from the sunlight. The eye was blinking and watering anyway.

36

All this for a jock chaser who was off on a yacht somewhere.

A stick rapped Jack's butt. He whirled, fists up.

"Move along, cowboy," said a police officer.

"Just waiting for somebody."

"I don't care if you're waiting for the rodeo, you
can't wait here." He hefted his brown club. "Join the
parade or clear the area."

Jack strode through the front gate into the park.

Inside, up close, the crowd broke into pieces, like a
jigsaw puzzle. Family groups, gay couples, a Black minis-
ter leading his congregation, a pack of Puerto Rican
Cub Scouts in full uniform. Teenagers on roller skates
and a group of senior citizens carrying their own folding
chairs. Most of them were wearing I LOVE THE SOUTH
BRONX buttons. Jack was surprised to see so many different kinds of people in the South Bronx, looking healthy
and nicely dressed.

A man climbed to the platform, blew into the mike
and welcomed them to *I Love the South Bronx* Day. He
said that if the mayor didn't help the South Bronx, he
wouldn't be reelected. The crowd cheered. The man
introduced the band from Johnny Garcia's Musical
School for Youth. In a corner of the field, several dozen
kids began playing the theme from *Rocky* as people
spread blankets, opened picnic bags and handed out soda
cans.

Jack roamed the edge of the crowd. Twice, he started
toward tall, black-haired girls. Neither was Jillian.

One after another, speakers clattered up the metal ladder to the platform. A priest, a doctor, two politicians, the head of a store-owners' organization. They all seemed to be saying the same thing: If we work together, we can make life better in the South Bronx.

The noon sun was burning through Jack's clothes. He felt discouraged. Dumb. He started back toward the gate. He thought about buying a ticket to the double-header so the trip into the city wouldn't be a total loss. Or a total lie. On the other side of the street, the Stadium gleamed in the sun. Be something to go, he thought, knowing I'll be pitching there myself in only three more days.

He was almost at the gate when a deep roar burst out of the public address system. Jack stopped and turned. A dozen teenaged Puerto Ricans had stormed onto the platform. It shuddered and swayed and clanged as they stomped in double time on its metal floor. They chanted and thrust their fists into the air.

Suddenly, they fell silent and snapped to attention as one of them leaped out of the pack and seized the microphone.

"Whatsa matter with you people?" he shouted. "Don't you know the time for standin' around and singin' is over?"

The crowd murmured angrily. Jack moved back toward the platform to get a better view.

The speaker was short and powerfully built. Thigh muscles bulged through his shiny black pants. A satiny green shirt unbuttoned to his navel exposed a waffle grid of stomach muscles. Tattooed dragons and snakes writhed on his massive arms.

"It's time for action. No more beggin' downtown for a handout. We got to take back our own turf."

Fierce eyes, as black and hard and glittery as marbles, blazed out of a round, light-brown face. He had a scraggly mustache and beard. The sun winked off diamond chips in his earlobes. He looked no more than seventeen or eighteen, but those eyes, and the anger in his voice, reminded Jack of guerrilla leaders he had seen on TV.

"People are dying, just a few blocks from here. Old people, sick people, babies. What you gonna do about it?"

One of the politicians and the store owner began shouting at him to shut up and come down from the platform. The crowd booed. Jack's eye was caught by a flash of purple at the base of the platform. A black-haired photographer in purple overalls was shooting up at the speaker. He shouldered his way toward her.

"Why don't you go across the street and ask those politicians and millionaires in Yankee Stadium, 'How can you watch a baseball game while people are dying 'cause there ain't no money to . . .'" His lips were still moving, but there was no sound. Someone had shut off the public address system.

"Jillian!"

"Jack!" She turned in a swirl of black hair. She looked glad to see him. "Can you believe this? They're so afraid of Hector they pulled the plug on him."

"You know that guy?"

Police whistles shrilled. More people were yelling at Hector now, and some of them were shaking the support poles of the platform.

"He's the one I told you about, the one who invited me to come here."

The young Puerto Ricans were jumping off the platform and disappearing into the crowd. Hector was the last one off. He dropped to the ground beside Jillian.

"You still want to come?"

Jillian nodded.

The hard black eyes flicked over Jack. "Who's this guy? I seen him somewhere before."

"He's my friend." Jillian took Jack's arm. He shivered at her touch.

"You sure he ain't undercover?"

Jillian laughed. "Sure."

"Okay." Hector didn't look entirely convinced. He glanced over his shoulder at several advancing police officers. "Come on."

"You going somewhere with him?" asked Jack.

Jillian's cheeks were red with excitement. "Come with me?"

He scooped up the brown leather camera bag at her feet. "Why not?"

7

"You got to have imagination," said Hector. "You got to look at this pile of stone and see the future. You know what I mean?"

Jack nodded, but he wasn't sure. He saw a pile of dirty-gray stone, chipped and cracked, that had once been a handsome four-story apartment building. Most of its windows were boarded up or gaping blindly out on a street of burned-out hulks. The building rose out of the rubble of the block like a tombstone in a long-forgotten cemetery.

Jillian lowered her camera. "How come this building didn't burn down, too?"

"We spread the word," said Hector. "Anybody come to burn this building, they gonna eat their fire."

"Who would come to burn it?" asked Jack.

"Used to be mostly junkies," said Hector, "but now the landlords get pros to do it. Hire a fire."

"Why?"

"For the insurance," said Hector. "Where you been, man?"

The air was sour and smoky. Jack's eyes watered and stung. His clothes stuck to his body like athletic tape.

He watched Jillian check the light and frame each picture before she pressed the shutter. She seemed so skillful and confident with a camera in her hands, sure hands that moved gracefully over the levers and buttons and dials, adjusting the settings, changing lenses, switching cameras.

Hector was watching her, too. Jack didn't like the way Hector's eyes slid over Jillian's body. He didn't like Hector. Too arrogant. Hector snapped his fingers and six of his followers silently filed into the building. The other six stared at Jack. They made no sounds, they hardly moved, they seemed like ghosts in this dim, eerie neighborhood. Jittery feelings quickened Jack's pulse and prickled the hairs on the back of his neck, but he stared back at the six ghosts with the slit-eyed, tight-lipped expression he used to intimidate batters. Most of them looked to be thirteen or fourteen years old, girls and boys, dressed in jeans and T-shirts and sneakers. Jack remembered hearing a TV newscaster refer to sneakers in the ghetto as "felony boots." He wondered if he had made the mistake of his life by coming here.

"I'm finished out here," said Jillian. "Unless I could

42

make a shot of you and your gang in front of the building."

"This ain't no gang, man," said Hector, "not anymore. This is a collective of youth. Gangs got names and they wear special clothes to separate themselves from the people. We got no name and no special clothes and no membership list because we are the people."

"How about all of you lined up in front of the building?" asked Jillian.

Hector shook his head. "No pictures of us. It could fall into the wrong hands."

"Who are you afraid of?" asked Jack.

Hector's voice hardened. "We're not afraid of nobody, because we are right. The fat cats downtown are afraid of us because we are going to make them share the wealth."

"Like Robin Hood?" asked Jillian.

"Robin Hood was a sellout," said Hector. "Robin Hood stole from the rich and gave to the poor till the old king came back, and then Robin Hood kissed his feet like everybody else. We don't kiss nobody's feet."

He swaggered into the building. Jillian picked up her camera and followed him in. Jack followed Jillian, the six ghosts on his heels.

The ruined lobby stank of urine. The walls were covered with graffiti, carved and spray painted. Names, dates, warnings, curses, stick figures. Jillian activated her strobe light and shot the walls.

"What do you think?" asked Hector.

43

"People's art," said Jillian, without looking up.

"And you?" Hector's eyes narrowed as he turned to Jack. It was some kind of a test.

"Vandalism," snapped Jack.

Hector's lip twitched. "Where you live?"

"New Jersey. Why?"

Hector laughed, a nasty bark. "That figures. The landlords who pay to burn up the Bronx, they live in big houses in New Jersey."

"I don't know anybody like that," said Jack. The jittery feeling was draining away, just as it did when he stepped on the mound for the first pitch of a game.

"You might be one of them," said Hector. "You don't care what happens in the Bronx, you don't care if there's people in the house when you torch it. Just so long as you got your big cars and your giant-screen TV and your cowboy clothes. Far as you concerned, the Bronx is just Indian Territory."

"I think you're full of it," said Jack.

A hush, then small sounds. The whisper of Jillian's camera brushing her overalls as it dangled from her neck. The squeak of rubber soles as Hector's people shifted from foot to foot on the lobby's marble floor. His own rapid breathing.

Hector's eyes were very cold as they measured Jack. "That's what you think, huh?"

"Yeah." Jack felt his body prepare for action. Blood pumped. If it's a fair fight, he thought, if the others don't jump me, I'll have a chance. Hector looks stronger than me, but I'm at least eight inches taller. Much longer

44

reach. Weigh about the same. One quick punch in his face, put me on the offensive. Of course, if he's packing a gun or a knife . . .

"I don't think Jack meant that," said Jillian.

"I think this dude says exactly what he means," said Hector. "Don't you?"

"Yeah."

Suddenly, Hector began to chuckle. He shook his head. "Man, I can't believe how dumb you are, talk to me like you do, here, on my turf. Come on, I want to show you something."

Jillian looked at Jack and raised her eyebrows. He shrugged and followed Hector up the lobby steps into a dark, stifling hallway. Hector pushed open a door and led them into an apartment. They followed him from room to room.

Jack gagged in the bathroom and in the kitchen, small, hot, stinking boxes crawling with cockroaches and silverfish.

The bedroom was just large enough for two beds, one along each wall, separated by a sagging, splintery wooden chest of drawers. There was a brown plastic crucifix over each bed. The water-stained walls were covered with pictures cut out of magazines, pictures of flowers and snow-covered mountains and sandy beaches. The pathetic attempt to decorate the room made it seem even uglier and sadder to Jack.

He didn't see the two children right away because they were so small and so still. They sat together on one of the beds, their mouths slack, their eyes empty.

45

They didn't respond as Jillian smiled and said, "Hi, what are your names?" They barely blinked as her strobe light flashed.

In the sudden light, Jack noticed that both of them had ropes knotted around their waists. They were tied loosely to the radiator, like dogs on a leash.

Jack stepped out of the room to give Jillian more space to move around as she shot. Hector came out after him.

"Even gets to you, huh?"

"Where are their parents?" asked Jack.

"Just a mother," said Hector. "She had to go out to get more dresses to work on. That's how she survives, man, slaving for a pig who makes big dollars selling dresses she sews for pennies. High price dresses. For the downtown stores. Can you dig that?"

Jillian stumbled out of the bedroom. Tears streamed down her cheeks. "They don't even smile."

"What they got to smile about?"

"What can we do?" asked Jillian.

"Let's get them some food," said Jack. "Milk, bread, eggs, orange juice, green vegetables. Vitamins."

"Scraps off your table," sneered Hector. "You got to do better than that. You know how many kids in this city, this country, ain't getting what you had too much of all your life?"

"So what the hell are you doing about it?" Jack was surprised at how loud his voice sounded. "Those people at the rally were trying to get something going, and you just busted in with your big talk . . ."

46

"You got to be crazy, man," said Hector. "Is that how you got your eye all messed up, runnin' off at the mouth?" He peered up at Jack. "I know I seen you somewhere before."

"My pictures," said Jillian, quickly. "I'm going to show them to the Mayor."

"He don't care," said Hector.

"If he knew he'd care," said Jillian.

"C'mon," said Hector. "There's more."

Jack followed numbly. He looked into each of the other apartments that Hector opened, but the image of the two little children tied to the radiator, slack jawed and empty eyed, was superimposed on everything else he saw. A blind old woman reached out to touch Hector's face. A man who spoke no English broke into a wide smile when Hector poked his head through the door. He spoke too fast for Jack's classroom Spanish. There were other children, and some of the apartments were even worse than the first one. Broken pipes jutted out of jagged holes in crumbling walls. Cracked ceilings sagged and plaster dust fell like snow.

"I've got enough," said Jillian. Her voice quavered. "When the Mayor sees these . . ."

"He's gonna say, 'Nice pictures,'" mocked Hector. "He's gonna say, 'Too bad we ain't got no money for these poor spics, we spent it all on new hotels and Yankee Stadium and fixing up the roads so cowboys from New Jersey can get home quicker.'"

"Not after he sees these pictures," said Jillian. "He doesn't know what it's like . . ."

"He knows," said Hector. "That's why the fat cats got him elected. He knows and he don't care."

"Why are you giving her a hard time?" asked Jack. "She came here because she cares."

Hector's mouth fell open. He shouted. "Angel! Emira! José!"

Girls and boys rushed into the apartment. Jack thought he saw the dull metal sheen of a gun in one of their hands.

"What's wrong?" asked Jillian.

"I know who you are." Hector slapped Jack's shoulder. He spoke in Spanish. His people grinned at Jack and shook his hand and patted his back.

Hector's black marble eyes were dancing. "Hey, man, that was some kind of catch you made."

"You were there?" asked Jack.

"That's where I met Hector," said Jillian.

"Love baseball," said Hector. "You know, I played third on that Bronx Vocational team. Till I quit school." He snapped his fingers. His people left the apartment as quickly as they had come in.

"You got some pair on you, Jack, going over the fence like that." He chuckled. "I thought you looked real familiar. Explains everything, why you so cocky and so ignorant. Come on, now I'm going to show you something real special."

They had to hurry to keep up with Hector, down another dark hallway, up a flight of broken steps. Hector lit a match. A rat scurried away. Just before the match sputtered out, they reached a dead end, a locked steel door without a knob. Hector lit another match and opened the door with a key. It swung open to a cascade of sunlight. The roof.

While they stood on the threshold, Jack asked, "What did you mean, it explains everything?"

"Your head's been somewhere else," said Hector, punching Jack lightly on his left arm. "You're a jock. You don't know what's going down in the world."

8

"A couple months ago," said Hector, softly, "I came up here to hide from some guys. I was here all night. I watched the sun come up. First, I only could see this roof, all messed with birdstuff and junkie garbage, and then I could see the dead cars and the broken buildings on the street.

"And I looked past that and I could see the trees in the park and the kids going to school.

"I kept raising my eyes. The skyscrapers. When the sun hit the skyscrapers downtown, every window was like winking at me.

"And I stood right here, I swear this, it sounds crazy, but I felt like I was some kind of a god, I could reach out and touch the whole city, everybody in the city, and it was like a message. Premier Hector of the Satin

Devils is over, finished. You got to be Hector of the people, and you got to change the world."

Jack realized he had been holding his breath. Jillian was leaning against him, shaking.

"The Satin Devils was real hard to persuade. A serious gang, man, lots of pride. But most of them came out with me. I made them see it. I said, You want to end up a thief, a junkie, when you got a chance to make history?"

He motioned Jack and Jillian to follow him across the soft, shifting tar to a corner of the roof. He unfolded three plastic-and-aluminum beach chairs and dragged out a picnic cooler. When they sat down, he handed each a can of beer. He lifted an old piece of canvas covering a large portable radio and tuned in the Yankee game. "Welcome to my private club."

"What about those kids downstairs?" asked Jack.

"I got a dream," said Hector. "If we could take over this building and fix it up, we could give all these people a decent place to live. That's the first step to getting over in this world, a decent place to live where there ain't no rats in your bed and roaches in your cereal and junkies hiding out on the stairs waiting for you and there's heat so you ain't sick all winter and light so you can do your homework and get an education."

"What's stopping you?" asked Jack.

"The landlord. He still owns the house. He's waiting for the chance to burn it for the insurance."

"I read somewhere," said Jillian, "that there's a law that tenants can take over an abandoned building."

"It's real complicated," said Hector. "I checked it out. It could take years. Those kids don't have years. You see how they look. Who knows what's happening to their brains?"

"When the Mayor sees my pictures," said Jillian, "he'll want to help you."

Hector snorted. "Those fools at the rally think if you kiss the Mayor's foot he'll help you. I think if you kiss his foot he'll kick you in the teeth. Unless you're a land-lord."

"That's not true," said Jillian. "I know him. You could explain it to him personally. He could cut through all the red tape for you."

"Oh, man, just fifteen minutes with the Mayor, I'd make him see it, too." His eyes glittered. "If we could get this house fixed up, move some more people in, this could be a model for the whole South Bronx, the whole city. For other gangs. It could spread. You got to just keep raising your eyes, you know?"

As hot as it was, Jack felt chills through his body. He glanced at Jillian. He could tell she was affected, too.

"What about those kids downstairs?" asked Jack. "Could we do something for them now? I got some money on me . . ."

"No," said Hector harshly. "You got to understand. That's the problem. Rich people give poor people the scraps off their table, like they were dogs. That way, the rich stay rich and the poor stay poor. It's got to be different, this time. No handouts."

"But until you get the building fixed up . . ."

"That's why it's got to happen soon." Hector stood up. "I got to go. I can't stay in one place too long."

"Where do you live?" asked Jillian.

Hector's arm swept the horizon. "With the people. Like Zapata. Sandino. Like Fidel."

"You a Communist?" asked Jack.

"I be whatever I need to be," said Hector. "Now I go. You got to stay here till the second Yankee game is over. The minute you hear on my box it's over, go right downstairs. One of my people be in a red Pinto, take you back to the Stadium."

"Why all that?" asked Jack.

"Security. I don't want nothing to happen to you while you under my protection. Bolt the door behind me. Nobody be able to get up on the roof unless you let them in."

They walked Hector across the roof to the iron door. Jack pulled it open. It was hot to the touch.

"You gonna be here awhile, so make yourself comfortable," said Hector. "Pretend you at a nice beach somewhere. That's what poor people do."

He slipped through the doorway and was gone.

9

They lay on their backs, sipping beer and tracking clouds drifting across the sky. Jack had found an old blanket behind the cooler and spread it on a smooth patch of roof. He had stripped off his shirt and boots and socks. Jillian rolled up her overalls above her knees and slipped out of the shoulder straps. Their bare arms and their bare feet touched.

She turned on her side. "I was really glad to see you. But I wasn't surprised."

"You thought I'd show up?"

"I knew it."

"How come?" he asked.

"Because I wanted you to."

"You always get your way?"

Jillian laughed. "Hardly ever. But I knew this

time was going to be different."

He sat up to get a better look at her. Her hair was a black halo around her face. She reached up to touch his cheek and the bib of her overalls fell away. She made no effort to cover herself.

He leaned down to kiss her.

Her lips were very warm, very soft. She put her hands on his bare back and pulled him down. After a while, he felt as though he was melting into her.

The sun was dropping into New Jersey, beyond the rooftops to the west. The cool of the late afternoon tickled the damp hairs on his body. He turned up the Yankee game. Top of the seventh inning of the second game. The Yankees had a big lead.

"We have to go?" she asked sleepily.

"Not yet." He stretched. His right elbow buzzed, and he winced.

"What's wrong?"

"Nothing."

"Your arm hurt?" She raised her head. "Isn't that the arm you pitch with?"

"It's no big problem. I get shots."

"What kind of shots?"

"I don't know."

"How could you not know?"

"Painkillers, anti-inflammatories, the usual stuff."

"You just let the doctor shoot your elbow?"

"Hey, what's the big deal?"

She snuggled against him. "I like your elbow."

"I trust the doctor." The conversation made him uneasy. "He's the team doctor."

"There've been a lot of side effects with some of those drugs."

"How do you know so much about it?"

"I've read a lot about drugs. And Dr. Shaw's an authority on therapeutic drugs and he talks to us . . ."

"Who's Dr. Shaw?"

"He runs the commune. The entire concept is his idea."

"Is he a shrink?"

"Yeah. I think you'd like him. He's very smart. You should come visit."

"Okay, I will." He dropped back on the blanket. "How's tomorrow?"

"I'm going to spend the day developing and printing the pictures. Come in the evening after dinner. We have Presentation on Monday evenings."

"What's that?"

"One of the residents presents something, a show, a talk. Everybody comes, and Dr. Shaw's always there for Presentation."

"When are you going to take the pictures to the Mayor?"

"Let's see how they come out first."

"They're going to be fantastic," said Jack.

"How do you know?"

"I know." He reached for her.

"How much time do we have?"

"Two innings," he said.

56

10

He had always felt comfortable in Dr. May's waiting room among the trophies, cups and autographed balls the orthopedic surgeon collected from grateful patients. There was even something of Jack's on one of the shelves, a most valuable player plaque from a County All-Star tournament.

But this afternoon he felt strangely out of place. The room seemed to be pressing in on him. He was ashamed to exchange the usual nervous smiles with the others in the room, a man on crutches and a woman with a little girl. They were already in the room when he arrived, and he knew they would still be there when he left. Dr. May would take him first. Dr. May never kept an athlete waiting. Except, of course, for a more important athlete.

He had never thought of that before. Just accepted it. An image of the two little kids on the bed flashed through his mind. They should be seeing a doctor. He pushed the thought away and studied the photographs and letters on the walls. He had seen them all before. A pro soccer player gave Dr. May credit for extending his career. A college basketball coach whose team had won its conference wrote that Dr. May had been like a sixth man on the court. Dr. May's round face beamed out of the photos, always surrounded by athletes.

"Jumpin' Jack!" Dr. May bounced into the waiting room in red suede jogging shoes, his white doctor's coat flapping. He smiled and waved at his other patients as he shook Jack's hand and steered him into his private office.

"So?" Dr. May waved Jack into a leather chair and perched on a corner of his massive desk. He grinned. "Who told you to go into the stands after a foul? Where was the catcher? The first baseman? You a one-man team?"

"I had the best angle," said Jack.

"Angle." Dr. May made a comic face that wrinkled the smooth, shiny skin of his freshly shaved head. "You pitchers are a breed apart. All crazy. Contrary to popular belief, I think right-handers are even crazier than left-handers." He leaned forward and slapped Jack's knee. "Don't let anybody kid you, that was a very ballsy thing to do. You keep up that attitude of yours, Jack, you're going to be a big winner. On the field and off it."

His intercom buzzed. "Okay, sweetie." He jumped

off his desk. "You're up, Jack." He bounced out of the office. A nurse was helping an older woman inch out into the hall with a walker. "Lookin' good, Martha." said Dr. May. The woman gave him a weak smile.

Dr. May led Jack into the stark white and stainless steel examining room. "Let's look at that eye first."

He stripped off the tape in one quick motion and fingered the flesh around the wound. "Clean. How's the hinge?"

Involuntarily, Jack bent his right arm. No complaint from the elbow. "Feels okay."

"It should. You haven't pitched in a couple of days. Rest does it every time. That's what I prescribe for most of my patients, rest. I tell 'em to stay off the knee for a while, stop bending the elbow."

Dr. May grinned and shook his head. "The trouble with you jocks is you can't rest like real people, you've got to get back into the game right away. That's why I've got all these gray hairs." He ran his fingers through the air above his bare scalp. "Oooo-keee. Tell me when it hurts."

He began to pinch and poke the flesh around Jack's elbow. He bent the arm, rotated the hand on the wrist, felt all the way up to the shoulder and along the trapezius muscle. Jack said, "There," or "Yup" whenever he felt pain. He tried to remember how many times he had gone through this since the first time he had ever felt the deep elbow twinges that had scared him, that had signaled the kind of injury that could hamper or even end his pitching career. He had been thirteen when

59

he started seriously working on a curveball and a slider. Dad had shown him the grip and caught his pitches for hours in the backyard. Dad had said, Since you're going to do this anyway, you might as well do it right. The pain had started when he was fifteen.

"How'd it feel at practice this morning?"

"I didn't throw any breaking stuff. A little pain, but I was able to pitch through it."

"Well." Dr. May leaned against his examining table. "If you hadn't made that crazy catch and won the game, you wouldn't be pitching in Yankee Stadium the day after tomorrow. You'd be able to take the rest of the summer off and get that wing into shape. But you can't, so I might have to give you something new on Wednesday."

"What is it?"

"It's got a long name. How's your Latin?"

"What about side effects?"

"Don't panic, it won't make your dingus fall off." Dr. May grinned. "I hear you're a pretty good pitcher in that league, too. How's that little blond tennis player you were going around with last year?"

"Kristie? She's fine." He had tried not to think about her since Saturday night.

"Very pretty girl. Didn't she have some problem with her shoulder?"

"It's okay now. She's seeded number three in the county."

"What did she take?"

"Just heat and vitamins."

60

Dr. May shook his head. "I wish your case were that simple. But your elbow isn't responding properly to the Butazolidan anymore." Jack thought he made it sound as though his elbow wasn't trying hard enough.

"What are you going to give me?"

Dr. May sighed. "A special concoction. The basic ingredients are cortisone and xylocaine. . . ."

"Cortisone? That's a . . ."

"They're using it in the Bigs routinely," said Dr. May. "It's like a miracle. Hit the spot, twenty minutes later no pain."

"I've heard that cortisone can cause some . . ."

"Look, Jack, it's up to you." Dr. May cocked his head. "Answer me one question?"

"What's that?"

"Do you really want to pitch in Yankee Stadium?"

"Sure."

"Reach into yourself. I mean, psychologically, do you *really* want to pitch? Because if you're afraid, if you don't want to accept the responsibility, if you don't want to win, one way to avoid the whole thing is to come up with a sore arm. Who could blame you for that?"

"It's nothing like that," said Jack. But suddenly he wasn't sure.

"I've had a lot of experience with jocks," said Dr. May. "You'd be surprised how many of them don't really want to win. There's a lot of responsibility in being a winner. I always thought you were one of the winners. Am I wrong?"

Jack shook his head.

61

"I didn't think so. Ooo-kee. I'll examine you right before the game and decide if we'll shoot you or not. Got enough Darvon?"

Jack nodded.

"Any other questions?"

"No."

"Then take a hike, stud." Dr. May slapped him on the butt. "I've got sick people to take care of."

11

He got lost on the narrow, twisting streets of Greenwich Village and then spent a half hour finding a parking spot big enough for his creaky old Plymouth. A pearly gray twilight was sifting through the skimpy trees stuck in the sidewalk by the time he arrived at the brownstone where she lived. A high-pitched wisp of music curled out of a front window. He thought of spooky TV movies.

He pressed a glowing white button alongside the heavy wooden front door. A voice floated out of a black grid above the button. "Who is it?"

"Jack Ryder," he shouted into the grid.

"Who?"

"Jack Ryder. I'm visiting Jillian."

The doorknob buzzed and he opened the door into a vestibule. He caught a glimpse of himself in the glass of the inner door. He was glad he had prepped up for this trip, a blue shirt with a buttoned-down collar and blue cord slacks.

Jillian opened the inner door. Her hair was pulled back and tied behind her head with a black velvet ribbon. It made her face seem larger and younger than he remembered. She wore a red plaid blouse and balloony tan pants. It occurred to him that he had never seen her dressed in any color but purple before.

"Hi," she said softly, almost shyly, he thought.

He glanced over her shoulder, saw the hallway behind her empty, and leaned over to kiss her. She moved her head slightly, and his lips brushed her cheek. She didn't respond. Nothing.

"What's the matter?" he asked.

"Fine," she said, "Want to come in?"

He was surprised to realize that she was actually waiting for an answer. Did she think he had driven in from Nearmont to stand here in the doorway?

"Sure."

She turned and shuffled down a hallway paneled in dark polished wood. His cordovan loafers sank into a thick, patterned carpet. Pretty fancy, he thought. They reached half-closed sliding doors. He followed her into a big, dimly lit room.

About a dozen kids were sitting on a rug in the middle of a wooden floor. Their eyes were closed and they were swaying to the music of a recorder being played by a hairy little fat kid. Jack recognized the wispy music he had heard on the street.

Jillian left Jack standing and sat down with the others. She closed her eyes and began swaying, too. He felt like a fool, standing alone.

When his eyes became accustomed to the dimness of the room, he saw that several older people were sitting on leather couches and upholstered chairs set against the walls. They looked like parents and teachers to Jack. They smiled and nodded at the music.

One of them, a man in a suit and tie, waved to Jack and pointed toward an empty chair. Jack sat down.

He checked out the kids on the floor. Most of the guys were overweight or underweight, and they had sallow, pimply, indoor complexions. The girls weren't bad-looking. One of them, a blonde, reminded him of Kristie. Except for her posture. Even when she was sitting on the floor listening to music, Kristie kept a straight spine. This girl was slumped, her shoulders rolled forward, her back humped. They were all sort of slumped, he noticed. Jillian, too.

The music went on forever. It got worse. The musician's face was almost covered by his beard and his long hair. His mustache grew down over his lips and hid the mouthpiece of the recorder.

The music annoyed Jack, tickled the inside of his ears like bugs, made his palms itch. How could those kids on the floor keep smiling and swaying?

The concert finally ended. The hairy kid just took the recorder out of his mouth and laid it on his lap. It took a few seconds for everyone to realize it was over, and then a few more to unlock their cramped legs. They staggered up to hug the kid. Even Jillian. Jack felt a pang of jealousy. The hairy fairy.

Then he felt crummy. The kid wasn't much taller standing up than he had been sitting down, and some of the water on his face was tears. And I'm putting him down, thought Jack. What's wrong with me? Ought to go up there and hug him myself.

"You must be Jack. I've heard a lot about you." The man in the suit and tie was standing in front of him, hand extended. "I'm Dr. Shaw."

Jack stood up to shake his hand. "Hi." He wondered exactly what Dr. Shaw had heard about him. Some people told their shrinks everything.

"I'm glad you could come," said Dr. Shaw, as if he had invited Jack himself. He was a small, slim, handsome middle-aged man with a deep, soothing voice. "Do you think we might talk for a few minutes before you leave?"

"About what?" asked Jack.

"Fine. See you later." Dr. Shaw gave him a friendly smile and moved away.

Jillian shuffled over with a plate of chocolate chip cookies. She seemed shorter than he remembered her. Maybe it was the hunched-over way she was standing. "Let's sit down," she said.

He followed her into a quiet corner of the room and sat beside her on a couch. Most of the others were leaving the room. Two girls began playing a duet on a piano.

"How'd the pictures turn out?" he asked.

"What?" She looked at him blankly.

"The pictures you took yesterday."

"Oh." She thought for a moment. "I had to help make these cookies for Benjamin's concert."

Her eyes were empty. Windows in a house with no one at home. Her lips were slack. He thought of the eyes of the kids on the bed, zonked with hunger. Donnie's eyes when no one was talking to him, making him think. What was she on?

"You okay?" he asked.

"Fine. How're you?"

"Want to go outside, take a walk?"

"Where?"

"Anywhere? So we can talk."

"I have to stay here."

"Why? Does Dr. Shaw make you . . ."

"I want to. Have a cookie. I helped make them."

"No, thanks." His mouth was dry. He couldn't believe this was the same girl who had been with him on the roof. "What are you taking?"

"What?"

"Like tranquilizers or downers or something. You're acting like a zombie."

She blinked and licked her lips. "Got to go now."

"Why?"

She stood up. "Got to." She shuffled out of the room.

His neck and shoulder muscles tensed, a string of little spasms that chewed along under his skin. He took a deep breath, held it until his lungs were bursting, then let it out slowly through his nose. Got to get out of this place. Horror House.

Dr. Shaw was waiting for him in ambush in the hallway. He felt a moment of panic, but Dr. Shaw's hands were shoved into the pockets of his gray summer suit jacket, and his voice was low and pleasant. "We can sit on the stoop and talk. Nice night."

Jack felt a little better outside. Easier to breathe. He didn't sit, though, even after Dr. Shaw sat on the top step and leaned against the wrought-iron railing.

"You weren't expecting to see her this way," said Dr. Shaw.

"She's stoned," said Jack.

"Sedated," said Dr. Shaw. "She was extremely agitated when she came in last night."

"She was fine when I dropped her off."

Dr. Shaw just smiled and nodded. A car cruised past. The street suddenly went dark, as if the fading gray light had been switched off. The lack of conversation didn't seem to bother Dr. Shaw. He hummed along with the faint music of the piano duet. Jack wondered if it was part of his shrink's technique. Finally, Jack asked, "What's wrong with her?"

"Jill needs a great deal of support right now," said Dr. Shaw. "What she doesn't need is pressure."

"What's that supposed to mean?" Jack couldn't keep the hostility out of his voice. He didn't trust Dr. Shaw. There was something sneaky about him.

"I can't really talk about her," said Dr. Shaw. "Jill is a resident here."

"Jillian." It popped out of him.

"Yes, well, Jillian is an aspect of her personality that you have come to know."

"What do you mean? She's a split personality?"

"Jill is not a toy. You can't pick her up and put her down. She requires commitment. And you're a ballplayer. You have heavy responsibilties of your own. I hear you've got a big game coming up at Yankee Stadium."

"So what?"

"So you wouldn't want anything to happen because of you."

"Like what?"

Dr. Shaw sighed. It was too dark now to see his face clearly, but Jack thought he made out a frown. "You're pushing her, Jack. The pictures . . ."

"That was her idea."

"Right. An idea. But you tried to make it a reality."

"What's wrong with that?"

"She's not ready. That's what I mean by pressure. If you push her to do something that she isn't ready to do . . ." He let the sentence hang in the air, ominously.

"What could happen?"

"I don't know."

"You think she would kill herself?" He said it challengingly to cover the fear bubbling in his stomach.

"I can't discuss that," said Dr. Shaw crisply.

"What if I tell her not to go ahead with the pictures?"

"I suspect it's too late for that," said Dr. Shaw. "Jill wants to perform for you. She thinks she knows what will please you, what you expect from her. Achievement. Attaining an objective. Going the distance. Reaching the goal. The sports values."

"What's wrong with them?"

"She's not ready, Jack."

"You think I should just . . . disappear?" Jack was amazed to feel tears stinging his eyes.

"I think it would be best for her."

"Should I say anything to her?"

"It's not necessary. I'm here. There's a resident staff." Dr. Shaw stood up. "Good-bye, Jack. Good luck in your game."

They shook hands. Jack turned and started down the steps. He swallowed a lump in his throat, took a breath and turned back to ask Dr. Shaw if it would be all right to call her on the telephone sometime. Just to talk.

But Dr. Shaw had already gone back into the house and shut the door.

12

He always liked wind sprints. He would take his time warming up for them, fifteen minutes of stretching exercises, two or three easy laps around the field, then ten minutes more of hard stretches, thinking all the time of how good he would soon feel. He could get high on wind sprints. Blot out the rest of the world.

He started on the right field foul line, toes on the lines, elbows out to his sides, fists chest high, took a dozen deep, charging breaths the way Kristie had taught him. She was into yoga. He would wait until the light-headedness from the oxygen rush faded, then crouch and rock forward on the balls of his spiked shoes.

GO.

He exploded off the line and accelerated into top speed, driving himself forward until he felt every muscle

71

and organ in his body roaring toward total effort, one hundred percent of maximum, expanding, sucking up every drop of blood and air and calorie they needed to send him hurtling toward the center field fence. When he sensed he was pressing against his limit, he slowed, easing into a long, loping stride that let him pull up gradually, gasping. Walk and breathe, walk and breathe, until the acid evaporated from his muscles and the carbon dioxide blew out of his lungs and his body began to tingle and glow. In a minute his muscles began to beg for more.

He did six before he thought of Jillian and all the energy drained out of his body. He set himself for the seventh sprint, but he just couldn't pump himself to explode off the line.

He walked back to the right field fence and leaned against it. Except for a few early morning joggers on the cinder running track, the Nearmont High athletic field was empty. His favorite time of day for wind sprints. The sun had burned off the dew, but the air was still fresh.

He wondered if they all ate breakfast together in the commune.

Did Dr. Shaw sit at the head of the table?

Did he feed them their zombie pills with their orange juice?

He jogged home, a level mile on hard-packed dirt along the county road. The morning commuter traffic was building up. Neighbors climbing into their cars and kids setting off for summer school classes waved to him. He fixed a smile on his face and waved back. Once you're a winner you can't let down, you have to be friendly even when you don't feel like it or people get sore. They think you're stuck up. They never think you've got problems of your own.

By the time he got home, everyone was at breakfast. Mom and Dad exchanged glances as he walked in. Dad waved the sports pages. "The way the Yankees are going, you might end up pitching for them tomorrow."

"I'm ready," he said mechanically. It was what Dad wanted to hear.

"John?" prompted Mom.

Dad cleared his throat. "Uh, Jack, we just want you to know we're behind you one hundred percent. . . ."

"We know the kind of pressure you're under," said Mom.

"I'm okay." For one panicky moment he wondered exactly how much they did know. Jillian? Hector? Dr. Shaw?

"It's only a game," said Dad. He didn't sound as though he really meant it. "It's not as if Yankee Stadium's going to be the high point of your life."

"Not as long as you win," said Grandma.

Donnie lowered his glass. Milk clinging to the downy hairs on his upper lip gave him a white mustache. "You'll win, Jackie, don't worry."

"You bet." He winked at Donnie. Donnie, trying to wink back, blinked both eyes.

73

"So, what we wanted to say to you," said Dad, "was enjoy yourself. Hang loose. Don't sit around chewing your nails."

"John?"

"Actually, that's not what we wanted to say." Dad grinned sheepishly. "We just wanted you to know that whatever's been going on the last couple of days, and we're not prying, Jackie, you don't have to tell us anything if you don't want to, whatever it is, we're concerned, but we're still behind you."

"What *have* you been doing?" asked Grandma.

"Betty, please," said Dad. He waved Grandma quiet and looked seriously at Jack. "You're not in any trouble, are you?"

"Like what?"

"Is everything all right between you and Kristie?" asked Mom.

"She's not in trouble, you know, pregnant?" asked Grandma.

"No," said Jack.

Dad exhaled. His tone to Grandma was scolding. "Betty, you promised not to upset him," but Jack could tell he was relieved. It's almost funny, he thought, how far off-base they were.

"Maybe her being pregnant might not be the worst thing," said Grandma.

"What's that supposed to mean?" asked Dad.

"We still don't know exactly what Jack's been getting for his elbow . . ."

"For your information," said Dad, his face reddening,

"Coach Burg and Doc May have answered every question I've ever asked them."

"Maybe you're not asking the right questions," said Grandma. "I just recently read . . ."

"In *Prevention* magazine?" sneered Dad. He looked at his watch.

". . . they're finding more and more evidence that a number of long-term side effects, including sterility, can be traced to abuses in sports medicine."

"You don't really believe that Coach Burg or Doc May would . . ." began Dad.

"Coach Burg wants to win," said Grandma, "and what do doctors know? Only what the drug companies tell them. Look at Thalidomide, DES, all these additives, PCB . . ."

"I've got to go." Dad jumped up. "They're going to blow their corks when they find out I'm taking off early again tomorrow."

"Don't forget your Maalox," said Mom. She stood up to walk Dad to the door.

"Please, Betty," said Dad, "let's not have any more of these discussions until *after* Jack's game. It can only upset him."

Jack waited until he heard the front door close before he looked at his grandmother. She was staring down at her plate, lips pursed.

"It's okay, Grandma," said Jack. "I know you wouldn't bring it up if you didn't think it was important."

She reached out to touch his cheek. "Oh, Jack, you've always been such a good person."

"What about me?" asked Donnie.

"You're my best boy." She squeezed Donnie's arm with her other hand, but she never took her eyes off Jack. "You've always worked so hard, Jackie, you've been so good and kept everything to yourself and I know how important this game is to you, to the whole family, but Jackie, honey, one game isn't worth your future health . . ."

"We don't even know for sure the drugs are harmful," said Mom, reentering the kitchen.

"Are you definitely getting an injection tomorrow?" asked Grandma.

"Doc May said he'd decide before the game."

"Don't let him do it without talking to one of us," said Grandma. "Would you promise me that?"

Jack shrugged. "I don't know."

13

"Yankee Stadium." Coach Burg said the words so softly that Jack, sprawled across a bench in the back of the locker room, could barely hear them over the heavy breathing of his teammates.

"Yankee Stadium," the coach repeated, reverently, as if he was praying. "A dream come true."

Suddenly his voice rose, steely. "Some dream." Heads jerked up. "It's gonna be a nightmare tomorrow, the way you looked out there today. Where's your pride?"

Jack watched his teammates stir in the steaming base-ment locker room. It was even hotter in here than it had been on the field, and there was no fresh air. The players had just enough energy left to roll their eyes at each other and flip fingers at the coach under their legs. A few of the guys groaned. Joey DiNola blew a tremendous fart, his specialty.

"Cute, real cute," said Coach Burg. "And that's just what they're gonna say about you tomorrow." He let his hand dangle from a limp wrist. His voice ascended to a nasty falsetto. "Those pussies from Nearmont High are real cute."

"C'mon, Coach," muttered Todd Newman, "it's murder in here."

"You'd rather be a loser, Todd?" growled the coach. "So you could stay home in your air-conditioned den, watching the Flintstones, drinking Coke . . ."

"Drinking beer," said Bucky Flynn.

"Snorting coke," said DiNola.

The team cracked up, whooping, banging lockers, slapping palms. Jack laughed. Even the coach grinned.

"Good one, Joey, we all needed that, a little chuckle to loosen us up. Because we were flat out there. No hustle. No follow-through. No second effort."

"We'll get it together," said DiNola. "At the Stadium."

"It doesn't happen just because you want it," said the coach. "You've got to work at it. You know, Jack Ryder was out here this morning at seven o'clock running sprints."

Jack ducked as the guys hissed at him and a damp jockstrap came flying at his head.

"That's right, girls," said the coach. "This fella's not just wishing for it. He's willing to pay the price."

"That's 'cause he's not human," shouted DiNola. "Ryder's a robot."

"Okay." Coach Burg held up his hands. "Stay out of the sun this afternoon, drink plenty of fluids,"—he winked—"but no beer, please. Eat light. Rest."

"I got a hot date," yelled DiNola.

"Go to bed early tonight," said the coach. "Alone. This is the big one. Remember, we're never going to be all together again. So let's go out like champs."

They fell silent. Jack knew they were all thinking the same thing. We're a good team, and this is it. The last game for the seniors. Who knows how good we'll be next season. And what a way to end it. With the Metro Area Championship in Yankee Stadium.

"Bus leaves from the front of the school at one P.M. sharp. See you tomorrow." He clapped his hands. "Brian! Get your managers up here, front and center."

Jack took his time getting off the bench. He had thrown at half speed, but even that had aggravated his elbow. It nagged him now like a toothache. Everybody else had nonchalanted it through batting practice and the fielding and base-running drills, but he had pushed himself until he thought his bones would melt. It was the only way he knew to keep his mind empty, to avoid thinking of Jillian.

"How's the arm, Captain Perfecto?" DiNola was peering up at him.

Jack just shrugged. No answer was necessary. He knew the question was Joey's way of making up for the wise-guy crack to the coach, of reminding Jack it was nothing personal, just part of his self-appointed role as the team clown.

Todd pushed up. "Who's your press agent?"

Jack ignored him. Todd said the same thing every time Jack got a write-up in the paper or a compliment from the coach. Kristie used to say that if envy could really turn you green, then Todd would be the world's biggest frog. Kristie. She'd said a lot of smart, funny things. Why does she seem so blurry, so far away in my mind?

"Can't even do a couple of lousy wind sprints without making sure the whole world knows about it."

DiNola stepped between Todd and Jack. "C'mon, Todd."

"You think you're the only guy on this team, Jackoff?"

DiNola signaled Jack to leave. He turned back to Todd. "Maybe if you did a wind sprint once in a while, spaz, Jack wouldn't've had to nearly bust his head going after your ball."

They started to scuffle. Jack kept moving right out of the locker room. Someone would break it up fast, someone always did.

Coach Burg caught him at the door. "Nice workout, Jack. You all set for tomorrow?"

Jack nodded.

"Good. You're a blue-chip boy and you're gonna be some kind of a man. I know it and your folks know it, and your friends know it, and tomorrow, Jack, the whole world's gonna know it. There'll be scouts and VIP's and press and you name it at the Stadium. I hear the Mayor's going to throw out the first ball. That means extra TV. What did Doc say about the elbow?"

80

"He said he'll examine it at the Stadium."

"I better give him a call." Coach Burg patted Jack's butt. "Go home. Rest it. This is the Super Bowl, the Seventh Game of the World Series, the Gunfight at the O.K. Corral. After tomorrow, there's no tomorrow."

14

The house was empty when he got back from practice. He drank a quart of orange juice before he ate the two tuna salad sandwiches Grandma had left for him in the refrigerator. That's Grandma, he thought, you can always count on her for sandwiches or an opinion. Wonder how long that's going to last. The way she and Dad have been getting along, she's probably sorry she sold her house and came to live with us. Be too bad if she leaves. Mom seems a lot happier now that she's working at the Needleworks Shop and everybody seems a little less tense about money.

He was picking through the fruit bowl on the kitchen counter when he spotted the note to him in Grandma's beautiful old-fashioned handwriting. It read: "That girl called." There was a familiar phone number with a New

York City area code. Grandma's way, he thought. She was too honest not to leave the message, but she wasn't going to put it on the memo board where he would see it right away. He tore up the note.

He went upstairs with a peach and a banana. Stretch out. A little Willie and Waylon. He punched in a cassette. The elbow buzzed.

Maybe Grandma was right. She read all those health and natural living magazines. Be something, wouldn't it, after all these years of turning down joints and angel dust and greenies and ludes to find out that what Doc May's been giving me so I can pitch is making me sterile or messing up my kidneys or starting a cancer someplace. How can Doc May keep up on all the new research—he's always going to a game someplace. And Coach Burg. If Nearmont wins tomorrow, he'll be County Coach of the Year. Maybe State Coach.

The cassette snapped off. He hadn't heard a single song.

The glowing red numbers on the digital clock read 2:17 P.M.

A long time to dinner. Nothing on the tube. Everybody's over at the Swim Club. Might even work an hour or two. Could use the money. At least I could hang out with Eric and the guys, kill some time.

But Kristie would be there. That's not something I want to deal with right now. Take care of that *after* Yankee Stadium. Besides, Coach said to stay out of the sun. Makes you tired. Dehydrates you.

The phone rang and he automatically picked it up.

"Hello?"

"Jack?" It was Jillian.

His heart turned over. Just like a pancake. The dumb old cliché was true.

"Jack? It's me. Jack, are you . . ."

He hung up.

He was breathing hard. Sweating.

The phone rang again.

Let it ring.

Pick it up. Dr. Shaw didn't say anything about not talking to her if she calls you.

It rang at least thirty times before he jumped out of bed and grabbed his swim trunks and car keys and ran downstairs. It was still ringing when he left the house.

15

"Free advice from your big brother?" Eric didn't wait for an answer. "Kristie is a very special lady. You've got to treat her with respect and finesse."

"Thanks, I'll always remember that," said Jack.

"Do I detect sarcasm? Not your style, Captain Clean." Eric leaned back in the wooden booth and flexed his pecs for two girls walking through the snack bar. "Now, I can understand how a guy wants a taste of the strange stuff now and again. Natural. Human. Proves that even Jumpin' Jack cannot live on ball alone. But you do not flaunt it in your old lady's face, not if she's a winner like Kristie. Look at her out there."

Jack followed Eric's index finger. Kristie was sitting at the edge of her high chair overlooking the kiddie pool. She looked good. Her blond hair was dazzling in the afternoon sun. Her long, lean athlete's body was poised to leap into the water. Twice, while they watched her, she blew her whistle to stop horseplay. She took her job seriously. Jack liked that about her.

Eric reached across the laminated table to knuckle Jack's chin. "Little bro, you need me. You have lost your usual cool. A bimbo in a limo shows up and you . . ."

Anger scraped Jack's stomach. "I got to go. Coach said to stay out of the sun."

Eric leaned over and pushed him down. "Forget it. Old Burgoo is probably sprawled out right now in his backyard, greased like a pig, trying to get a tan for his interview."

"What interview?"

"Didn't you know? He's up for the Harrison University job. The baseball coach is retiring."

"He won't be at Nearmont next year?"

"Not if he can help it," said Eric. "That's why tomorrow's so important to him. Big win at the Stadium could cinch the job."

"We were kind of counting on him for next year, help me choose a college."

"Don't worry about it," said Eric. "That's next year. We've got to concentrate on the here and now. You and Kristie. The delicate dynamic of my lifeguard team. I'm not going to let some freaky broad . . ."

"Jillian's no . . ."

"She tell you about the time she was carried out of The Last Disco? Amy Goodman remembers seeing a

86

picture of her in the paper."

He was angry and fascinated at the same time. He wanted Eric to shut up and he wanted to hear more about Jillian.

"Now, far be it from me to deprive my little brother of nooky. But a few hours after this flake appears, you have a fight with your steady, you disappear all day Sunday and again on Monday night, and the whole time you never call the girl you have been seeing daily for nearly two years. Is that cool? Is that suave? Is that what I taught you?"

"Why was she carried out of the disco?"

"Who knows. Probably dope. So let's bring peace." Eric stood up, looking pleased with himself. "Don't do anything till you hear from me."

"Wait, I . . ."

"Relax, I'm going to talk to Kristie for you. Pave the way. I'll send her over. Just be cool and sweet, little brother, everything's going to be just the way it was before the spit hit the pan. As my dear old dad would say."

Jack watched him stride out of the snack bar and across the concrete deck, smiling and waving at Swim Club regulars. Two years in college and Eric knows everything. Shouldn't have come over here. Should've just taken the phone off the hook.

Eric dashed across the sand and took a running leap up the side of Kristie's chair. He dangled by one arm like an ape as he gestured back at the booth. Kristie glanced over toward Jack, then shook her head. Her eyes never left the kiddie pool again as Eric talked. And talked. Twice, he looked back at Jack and shrugged.

Kristie was hanging tough, Jack thought. That's no surprise. She's got a lot of pride. She's a winner.

Jack had an urge to get up and leave.

And go where?

Back home to the ringing phone? Maybe to that brownstone in the Village, Dr. Shaw's Nuthouse? Or up to Hector's abandoned building in the South Bronx? Some choices.

Kristie finally nodded. Eric threw a triumphant fist up in the air and leaped off the chair. He hit the sand and held up his palms. "Sit tight, little bro," he shouted. "Kristie's coming."

And everything's gonna be just the way it was before the spit hit the pan.

"Hi, Jack." Kristie slipped into the booth opposite him. Her face was expressionless.

"How you doing?" Dumb dialogue, he thought.

"Not terrific." She looked directly at him. "I'd like to know why you didn't call."

"I was busy." He felt uncomfortable, on the defensive.

"That's not good enough."

"C'mon, Kristie." He was feeling annoyed. "It's too hot."

"To be sorry?"

He picked his words carefully. "I'm sorry you feel bad, I really am. Okay?"

"That's your best shot?"

"It's no big thing. I went into the city Sunday and I

ran into the girl who . . ."

"The bimbo in the limo. Just like that?" Her blue eyes seemed glazed with ice.

He took a deep breath and fought down an urge to tell Kristie never to use those words again. "And last night I went to this place where she lives, it's sort of a, I don't know, a halfway house or something, to see if she had my pictures, and she didn't, and I don't expect to ever see her again." He took another breath. He was surprised to feel a damp stinging in his eyes. I don't expect to ever see her again?

"And as far as you're concerned, that's the end of it?"

"Yeah."

"You don't think you owe me a fuller explanation?"

"We're not married, you know."

Kristie's face turned almost as white as the zinc on her nose. "What's that supposed to mean?"

"That I don't have to account for every single minute of my time." He sat up straighter.

Color began flooding back into her face. "If you expect me to just sit around while you go off and . . ."

"I'm not asking you for anything, Kristie."

That stopped her. She leaned back. Finally, in a small voice, she said. "Maybe you're right." Her face relaxed. She smiled.

After a while, he smiled back. He had forgotten how pretty she was. They had had lots of good times together. Maybe he could try to tell her some of what happened so she could understand.

"On Sunday," he said slowly, "I went to this abandoned building in the South Bronx . . ."

"With her?"

"Yeah, she was taking pictures to show the Mayor. The guy who took us was Hector, a Puerto Rican guy who used to be gang leader, but now he's working to improve conditions up there."

"Why were *you* there?" Her brow wrinkled.

"That's a long story. What I want to tell you . . ."

"I'd like to know how you happened to be there."

He swallowed down his impatience. "There were these two little kids on a filthy, dirty bed, they were tied up so they wouldn't get hurt while their mother was out getting dresses to sew, that's how they survive." He sensed he had captured his audience. Kristie's eyes widened, and her face softened. "I never saw anything like it. Their eyes, like they were stoned. They didn't even blink when Jillian used her flash."

Kristie's eyes narrowed, but he could tell she was fighting her jealousy. And she was interested. "What would happen if there was a fire, and the kids were tied up?"

"Hector and his people were guarding the building, especially for fire. He says the landlord might try to torch it for the insurance. Hopefully, after the Mayor sees Jillian's pictures he'll help Hector take over the building."

"And you just went along to carry her cameras, huh?" Her lips were twisted. She had lost her fight.

He sagged back in the booth. He didn't feel like talk-

90

ing anymore. He drew a circle in a wet spot on the tabletop. He was glad when she finally said, "Got to get back."

He watched her slide out of the booth. She paused, as if waiting for him to say something, and when he didn't, she shrugged and walked away, up on her toes, with that high bounce she used walking on and off the court during tennis matches. The spectators loved it. Her hair rippled up and down like blond bird wings. She passed Eric on the sand. He took one look at her face, expressionless again, and started back up to the snack bar.

Jack left the Swim Club. He ignored Eric shouting his name.

He was driving home when an image flashed through his mind. The long black limo with the official New York City license plates would be parked in the drive-way. The chauffeur would be dozing at the wheel. Jillian would be sitting on the deck, waiting for him.

He stamped on the accelerator, then eased off. You *have* lost your usual cool.

From the end of the street he could see that his drive-way was empty. No cars at all. And the deck was empty, too.

It wasn't until he was pulling into the driveway that he saw Jillian, sitting on the front steps.

16

All he could think of to say was, "You're back in purple."
She was wearing the purple jump suit she had worn
the first time he saw her.

She laughed, the deep, throaty laugh he remembered.
Her eyes were bright and clear. "I didn't think you
noticed. Purple's my color. It gives me strength. It
matches my spirit."

"You weren't wearing purple last night."

"That's why I came out today. I didn't want that to
be the last time you ever saw me. Are you going to
invite me inside?"

"Oh, sure, sorry." He unlocked the front door and
led her into the living room. She followed so closely
that when he turned, they bumped. He felt her breath
on his face. The drapes had been drawn against the

sun, and the room was warm and stuffy and dim.

"Where's everybody?" she asked.

"Mom and Dad are at work. Grandma took Donnie to a special summer workshop. He's learning to make things."

"I want to see your room," she said.

"Upstairs." He took her hand and led her up the steps.

"It's like a museum. Are all these trophies yours?"

"Most of them don't mean anything." It was the first time he had ever said that. Had ever thought that. "I give a lot of them away. Would you like one?"

"No. Not if they don't mean anything." She looked around the room. She studied the poster of Jack and Kristie clowning on the beach. Lisa Curry had taken the picture last summer at the Shore and had two copies blown up into posters. "Is that your girl friend?"

"Yeah."

"She's gorgeous. She looks like a model."

"She models sometimes."

"You ever . . . make it with her here?"

He nodded.

"Let's go somewhere else," she said.

17

"It's beautiful here," she said.

The reservoir had never looked lovelier to him. It sparkled in the afternoon sun. A flight of ducks, a dark V in the blue sky, grew larger, skimmed the trees and settled, chattering, on the water.

Jack laughed. "When I first started coming here, with my grandfather, I'd ask him what the ducks were saying, and he told me I was too young to understand, they were telling dirty jokes."

Jillian laughed. "He sounds like fun."

"He was. One of those guys who could do anything with his hands. He built me a tree house once, he taught me how to fish. Those trees and bushes around the deck? He and I planted every single one of them. I was six that summer. I loved working in his garden. After a while, when he got too sick, he'd sit in his chair at the edge of the garden and tell me what to do. He called me his 'hands.' He'd tell me stories while I weeded. He'd been all over the world, he was a radio operator on merchant ships when he was young. I remember once, he was telling me about being attacked by pirates near Hong Kong, it was so exciting I just sat in the middle of the garden picking tomatoes off the plants and stuffing them in my mouth." Jack felt surprised and pleased. He never talked this much. It felt good.

"He used to come to all my games. He was a real fan. When Dad starting working out with me in the backyard, Grampa would be our cheering section. Dad got a real kick out of that, he said Grampa wasn't able to be around much when he was a kid, he was always looking for work. Dad liked the three generations all together in the backyard. My full name's John Scott Ryder the third. I must have cried for a week after Grampa died. I was in Little League then. I never knew my father's mother, she died before I was born. That was my mother's mother who worked you over on Saturday, she can be one tough lady, her husband died real young and she brought up my mother and her two sisters and a brother all by herself." He stopped. "Hey, I'm really running off at the mouth today."

Jillian reached out to comb his hair with her fingers. "I want to know all about you. I've got a million questions."

He felt wonderful. "Ask anything."

95

"Why did you hang up on me?"

He looked away. He had to think this through. He had never felt so close to her, closer than he had ever felt to any girl. He couldn't lie to her. He picked his words very carefully.

"A couple of years ago, before my grandmother came to live with us, we checked out some places for Donnie to live. He wasn't making much progress and the strain was really getting to Mom. Some of the places were pretty nice, clean and cheerful-looking, the doctors and all seemed okay, but the patients, they all had the same empty look in their eyes. Zombies. Nobody home."

He turned back to her. "Those kids in the Bronx. They had that look. So did you. It really got to me. Then, when Dr. Shaw told me that you . . ."

She broke in. "Dr. Shaw told you if you didn't leave me alone I'd commit suicide and it'd be your fault."

"Well, he didn't exactly come out and say it like that, but that's what he meant. Did you ever try?"

"Once, a long time ago. Dr. Shaw just wanted to scare you off. He doesn't like competition." She laughed when his head jerked up. "Not that way. For control of my head. Shrinks hate it when you're involved with someone else."

"How long've you been there?"

"About two months. My parents and I were having our problems, and then I got into some trouble."

"The Last Disco?"

"How'd you hear about that?"

"Somebody told me. It was in the papers."

96

"They blew it up because of my folks and the Mayor. They made me look like some crazy doper. Actually"— she grinned—"it was my diet pills that did it. I got a little nutsy."

"Why?"

"Pressure."

"That sounds like Dr. Shaw."

She nodded. "He's helped me see a lot of things. When I ate all those pills and went nuts I was declaring emotional bankruptcy. I was screaming for help. I was saying, Hey, world, I can't handle my problems anymore. You do it for me."

"What were your problems?"

She rumpled his hair and started combing again. "You've got a million questions, too."

"I want to know all about you, too."

That seemed to please her. She squeezed him. "Okay. I was in the Walton School, in Manhattan. You ever hear of it? No? It's like, if you don't make it at Walton, you don't make it. It was my fifth private school. My folks were up the wall. They promised to let me go to the U.C.L.A. Film School if I graduated from Walton. That's what I really want to get into, independent film production.

"So, two weeks before graduation, I was set to make the honor roll and everything, boom, I blew myself out of the water. Dr. Shaw calls it acting out. I ate all those pills because I was afraid of facing up to the responsibility of going all the way, of performing like an adult, of going out to U.C.L.A. and actually doing what I said I

97

wanted to do." She blew her nose and wiped her eyes. "Damn."

He sat up and put his arm around her shoulders. She tilted her head until it was resting on his chest.

The ducks finished feeding and started chattering again. They rose in a storm of wing flutter that sounded like applause and flew away into a darkening sky. He was glad he had never come here with another girl. But why hadn't he? He thought of Kristie. She would have liked it. Had he been saving the reservoir for Jillian?

They watched the sun slip into the far end of the reservoir, a bright orange ball into pale blue water.

"Doesn't it seem like it should sizzle going in?" she asked.

"Jillian? Sunday night, when you went back to the house and let Dr. Shaw give you those tranks. Were you doing the same thing? Giving up?"

"I don't think so. He said I was very agitated when I came in. I thought I was feeling terrific, but he said he thought I'd go into another psychotic episode, another mad scene like The Last Disco."

"Well, what I mean, do you think you were afraid of developing the pictures and taking them to the Mayor? Of going all the way, going the distance?"

"That's heavy."

"It would be a lot of responsibility, a lot of pressure, seeing that all the way through."

She peered up at him, smiling. "You really amaze me, you know that?"

98

"Why?"

"Because you're so smart and sensitive under all those muscles and clean-cut looks. You're not just a jock."

"Jocks don't have to be dumb. So, when are you going to develop the pictures?"

"Soon."

"How soon? Jill."

"Why'd you call me that?" Her head came up. Her smile was gone. "You know I don't like it."

"Dr. Shaw calls you Jill. He says it's an aspect of your personality. I guess Jill's the one who always quits in the clutch."

"Tonight." Her voice was excited. "All right? Tonight. I'll stay up all night and develop and print them. What do you think of that?" She was smiling again.

"I think it's a good start."

"A start?"

"Well, sure. When are you going to show them to the Mayor?"

"I don't know, I . . ."

"Why not tomorrow?"

"Tomorrow." She caught her breath. "Come with me?"

"I've got a game."

"That's in the late afternoon. We could go in the morning."

He hesitated. He should rest tomorrow until game time. He thought of Hector and the two little kids. They'd survived this long, they could survive one more day. He looked at Jillian. Her eyes were wide. She was waiting for his answer. He had pushed her this far . . .

"What time?" he asked.

Her smile was dazzling. "Could you meet me at seven? On the steps of City Hall? Can you find it?"

"Sure."

"I better get going," she said. "What time's the next bus leave for the city?"

"I'll drive you back."

"I got out here by bus, I can . . ."

"I want to. We'll have more time together." Gently, he pushed her down to the warm grass. "Jock and Jill."

"Jill and Jock," she corrected softly.

"Either way," he said. "So long as we get up the hill together."

100

18

His parents rushed out of the den as he tiptoed into the house. He could hear Johnny Carson's voice on the television set they had just left. It must be around midnight.

"Where the hell you been?" asked his father.

"I had something to do." He started up the stairs, but Grandma blocked the way. For once, all three of them are working together, he thought. Now, that's an upset.

"We've been very worried," said Mom. "No call, no note."

Why not tell them, he thought. "I drove Jillian back to the city."

"She was out here?" asked Mom.

"Yeah."

"Did you invite her?"

"No."

"She just happened to be in the neighborhood," said Grandma, in her cutting tone.

"Will you please tell me what's going on," said Dad. He glanced at his watch. "In less than . . . sixteen hours, you're going to be pitching the game of your life."

He had a sudden urge to dump it all out. Most of it, anyway. What he thought they could handle. Sunday in the Bronx and Hector and the kids in the abandoned building. The pictures for the Mayor.

He hesitated. What if they took it badly or started arguing among themselves? He was in no mood for a hassle.

"I'm just doing what you told me, Dad. Hanging loose." He kept his voice sweet and dumb, no reason to get Dad angry. "You said you didn't want me sitting around chewing my nails."

Dad looked at Mom and shrugged, but she wasn't satisfied. "Jack, something's going on here and I . . ."

"Jean," said Grandma, "let him get his rest. This can keep until after the game."

Another upset, thought Jack. Grandma bailing me out.

"Good night, Mom," He grabbed the banister and swung down to kiss her cheek. "Big day tomorrow." He threw a wave at Dad and jogged up the stairs.

As Grandma stepped aside to let him pass, she whispered, "Don't forget. Before you let them give you a shot." He gave her a kiss, too, but didn't answer.

He set his alarm for five-thirty and stripped. He was

suddenly exhausted, every muscle in his neck and shoulders aching.

But he couldn't sleep. What if he was pushing Jillian too hard and too fast? What if she cracked under the pressure? What if she . . . ?

He shoved it out of his mind.

What if her pictures were no good? After all this, what if they're out of focus or too dark to make out the kids' eyes or too light or blurry because her hands were shaking when she clicked the shutter?

Jillian had said she used her cameras as a reason for being somewhere. What if there hadn't even been film in the cameras? She just clicked away with empty cameras. Part of her therapy.

The last time he looked at the glowing red numbers on his clock they read: 2:37. An instant later, the clock was ringing.

He showered and shaved carefully. Got to look good. The swelling around his left eye was almost gone, although the skin was still purplish. That's all right. Purple's her color. He would have liked to blow-dry his hair, but the gun made too much noise and he couldn't risk waking them up. It would be tough to convince even Donnie that he was going out to jog in his navy-blue blazer and a striped tie.

He left a note on the kitchen table: WENT TO SEE THE MAYOR AT CITY HALL. MEET YOU ALL AT STADIUM. LOVE, JACK. That should hold them.

It was at least an hour before the full-scale commuter rush, but traffic on the Parkway was already heavy and the air was foul. No wonder Dad complained. He had to commute every day to a job he didn't like, a job he couldn't quit because he had a son who was one year away from college and another son who would need financial support for the rest of his life.

No wonder that game at Yankee Stadium means so much to him. If I can pitch my way through college . . .

At the tollbooth at the entrance to the George Washington Bridge he got directions to City Hall and he repeated them over and over aloud all the way down to his exit near the southern tip of Manhattan. The day was coming up hot. His clothes were soggy and exhaust fumes stuffed his nostrils.

He parked at an outdoor lot within sight of City Hall. He had to pay in advance. There wasn't much money left in his wallet. Gas and tolls for three trips into the city in the past three days had used up most of the ready cash that was supposed to carry him until he started getting paid at the Swim Club.

He spotted Jillian before she saw him. A purple skirt and jacket over a white blouse. She was sitting tensely on the City Hall steps, clutching her brown leather camera case. The photographs must be in the big, outside zippered compartment, he thought. Please, let them be good.

She jumped up. "I didn't recognize you from a distance, all dressed up." Her eyes were red rimmed and tired, but clear.

"How'd the pictures come out?"

"I didn't have time to mount them or anything. Some

of them are barely dry." She was nervous. She fumbled at the zipper. "I don't know, they're grainy, the film might have been out of date, they're overexposed, I think there's something wrong with my light meter . . ."

His heart sank. Too many excuses. He reached down to help her with the zipper. Her fingers were cold.

They opened the zipper together. A desperate, ripping sound. A manila envelope fell out of the compartment. He picked it up and tore it in his haste to get at the pictures.

They stunned him. They brought back the apartment building more vividly than his memory. He could smell again the stench of unwashed clothes and wasted bodies and rotting food and he could taste again the burning air and feel the grit settle on his skin. The back of his neck prickled.

"You did it, Jillian, you really did it."

She moaned with pleasure.

It was all there. The vacant stare in the childrens' eyes and the pathetic attempt to brighten the walls with magazine cutouts and the grimness of the buildings rising out of the moonscape of the block.

A warmth spread through him. He was proud of her.

She wasn't just talk. She was good. She could bring it.

He kissed her.

"What was that for?" She was grinning.

"Because I . . ." The words I Love You formed in his brain. He had never said them before, not to Kristie, not to any girl. The words melted and vanished on the tip of his tongue. "Because your pictures are fantastic."

"You really think so?" Her dark eyes danced.

"Didn't I tell you they were going to be?"

"I hope the Mayor thinks so."

"He will," said Jack. "They'll knock his socks off."

19

The Mayor was jogging in a blue velour running suit on the rubber-surfaced treadmill of a machine that recorded his speed, the distance he covered and his heartbeat. He was also dictating memos, letters, reminders, orders, to a man with a clipboard and a woman with a tape recorder and a calendar.

"C'mon, Jillie," said the Mayor over his shoulder, as Jack and Jillian were ushered into his little office gym, "we're running to the Statue of Liberty today."

"I always knew you could walk on water."

"That's funny, honey." He patted her on the head as she began jogging in place beside the machine, the manila envelope of photographs clutched against her purple jacket.

The Mayor turned toward Jack. "You run with us, too. What's your name?"

"Jack Ryder."

"That's a familiar name," said the Mayor. "Do I know your father?"

"He's the one Jillie slugged the other day," said the man with the clipboard.

"You signed a release, didn't you?"

"He's not going to sue," said Jillian.

"I never thought so." The Mayor reached out and patted Jack's head. "It's about three miles to the Statue of Liberty. It's always easier to run on these infernal machines when you think you've got a destination."

"How about the South Bronx?" asked Jillian.

"That is not funny," said the Mayor.

"I've got something to show you." She opened the envelope and pulled out a photograph of the two children on the bed.

"Nice shot," said the Mayor, enthusiastically. "You really are getting good."

"Is that all you can say?"

"You're terrific. Sooooo-per."

"No. About these children. They live in New York." She glanced over at Jack for support. He gave her a nod of encouragement. "You're their Mayor and they need your help."

The way she said it, in a flat, hard tone Jack had never heard from her before, seemed to rock the Mayor. He lost a step on the treadmill and had to speed up to keep pace. After he had recovered, he turned on Jack. "I thought you were an athlete. With big-league potential. What are you getting mixed up in this for?"

"I was with her when she took the pictures," said Jack. "It's pretty awful up there."

"I know, I know." The Mayor pulled a long face and nodded. "It keeps me up nights, kids, it really does. Where am I going to get the money for all the things that need to be done? If I could solve these kinds of problems, I wouldn't run for Mayor, believe me, I'd run for God."

"There is something you can do." As Jillian talked, she pulled out the rest of the photographs and held them up, one by one, in front of the Mayor. "There's a group of young people who want to take over this building and fix it up."

"There are agencies, Jillie. City agencies. Have them contact the appropriate . . ."

"It'll take too long. If you could just reach out and . . ."

"Jillie, if I do something as a favor for you, as much as I love you, the whole system breaks down. You've got to go through channels or you don't have a government." He looked at Jack. "I'm sure you understand, don't you, Jack?"

"Not really, sir," said Jack. "If you can't cut some red tape to help two little kids, what's the point of being Mayor?"

"You really play hardball, Jack." The Mayor chuckled. "What do you want?"

"If you could just meet with Hector, the leader,"

said Jillian, "for only fifteen minutes . . ."

"I'll give him ten," said the Mayor. "In my office tomorrow at . . ." He looked at the woman with the tape recorder and the calendar. "When do I have ten tomorrow, Charlene?"

She checked the calendar. "We could try to squeeze him in at twelve-twenty, right before your lunch with the Park Avenue Ladies' Garden Club. Your wife could . . ."

"Done," said the Mayor. "This Hector. What does he call his organization?"

"It doesn't have a name," said Jillian. "He said he doesn't want to separate it from the people."

"Hoo boy." The Mayor rolled his eyes. "You hear that, Al?"

The man with the clipboard snickered. "Another grassroots coalition."

"No," said Jack. "They used to be a gang, the Satin Devils, but they've reformed and . . ."

"Gang?" The Mayor signaled to Al, who twisted a dial on the machine. The treadmill began to slow. "Jillie! What have you gotten yourself involved with now?"

Her voice was small. "They're really trying to make a difference up there."

"It could be a model for gangs all over the city," said Jack.

"I think I've heard of the Satin Devils," said Al. "One of those teenaged wolf packs. Into everything you can imagine. Mugging, chain snatching, arson . . ."

"Not arson," said Jillian quickly. "They're protecting

110

this house from being torched. By the landlord. For insurance."

"That old story." The Mayor stepped off the treadmill and began mopping his face with a towel that Charlene handed him. "If it wasn't for the landlords, there wouldn't be a single building in New York. Jillie, you got conned. Don't feel bad, happens all the time. A slick street hustler latches onto some naive do-gooders, sells them a phony power to the people . . ."

"Those little kids were real," said Jillian.

"Maybe, maybe not. Look." The Mayor patted her on the cheek. "You run along now. I've got a big day . . ."

"You've got to give them a chance, you've got to . . ."

"Got to?" The Mayor raised his eyebrows. His face hardened. For the first time, Jack could see the real tough customer his father liked so much on TV. "Does this latest doctor of yours know about all this?"

"Well, he . . . uh . . ." Jillian's voice trailed off. She licked her lips.

"Maybe you better talk all this over with him. Your parents are certainly paying him enough." His voice grew chilly.

Jillian was speechless. She was blinking rapidly.

Jack said, "She's right. Everything she told you, I was there, too, and she's right."

"And you." The Mayor whirled on Jack. "You don't even live in the city."

"So what?" said Jack. "Once you see something like

111

that house and those kids, you have to be some kind of a zero to just sit around and not try to help out."

Al said, "Okay, Jack, you've had your say, now the Mayor's very busy . . ."

"I'm not finished." Jack was pleased at how smooth he sounded. "This isn't like anything I ever did before, Jillian either, and maybe Hector did con us, I don't know, but those pictures are real and it does look like hell up there, and you're the Mayor, you would know if it's on the level or not, and if you met with Hector you could make your own decision."

"That's enough now." Al took a step toward Jack, but the Mayor waved him back.

"Look at this from my point of view," said the Mayor. "How can I start holding conferences with every little hoodlum who wants to see the Mayor? What kind of signal am I sending out to honest citizens? That I'm soft on crime?"

"But this is a special situation," said Jack. "Two little . . ."

"Every situation is special. I've got millions of lives to worry about."

"What if nobody knew about the meeting?" asked Jack.

"How?" The Mayor raised his palms. "In this fishbowl?"

Jack looked at Jillian. Her eyes were bright and she nooded him on. He felt stronger, surer of himself, like he did on the mound when he knew his fast one was working.

"This afternoon," said Jack, "right after you throw out the ball at Yankee Stadium . . ."

The Mayor glanced at Charlene. "Is that today?"

"At four-oh-five. The Metro Area Championship."

"Go on." The Mayor nodded at Jack.

"Hector could meet you at the Stadium . . ."

"Too many people around," said the Mayor.

"Outside the Stadium then," said Jack. "It could look like you just bumped into him. There's a little park across the street. He could be jogging or throwing a Frisbee, and you could walk in like you're inspecting it."

"What's your angle?" asked Al. "You figure to walk in with the Mayor and . . ."

"He's going to be pitching," said Jillian. "In the Stadium."

The Mayor's eyes bugged. "You're pitching today?" When Jack nodded, the Mayor continued, "And you're running around like this. You must really believe in this Hector."

"I do," said Jack.

The Mayor looked at Charlene. She screwed her dark-brown features into a scowl and shook her head, No. Al shook his head, too. The Mayor made a face and looked at Jillian. After a minute, he said, "You got a deal. Tell this Hector I'll give him five minutes. He's got to be inside that park, waiting for me at four-fifteen. All alone. I'm not going to meet with a gang, whether it's got a name or not." He shook Jack's hand, then kissed Jillian's forehead. "Now get out of here both of you, before I change my mind."

113

Neither of them spoke until they were outside on the City Hall steps.

"You were wonderful," said Jillian.

"It was your pictures that got to him," said Jack.

"I had no idea you could talk like that," she said.

"Neither did I. You must've inspired me." He loosened his tie and opened the top button of his shirt. He had sweated through the armpits of his navy blazer. His legs and arms felt heavy, his head was filled with marbles and his mouth with cotton. He felt as though he had just pitched nine tough innings. He looked at his watch. Less than eight hours to the real game.

20

"You think I'm crazy?" asked Hector. "Or just stupid?"

His voice boomed in the dim, ruined lobby of the building. He stood above Jack and Jillian, at the top of three cracked marble steps, his massive, tattooed arms folded across his chest. Jack had the feeling he was orating for the benefit of the shadowy figures in the corners.

"You think I'm just gonna walk into that trap?"

"It's no trap," said Jillian. "It's a chance for you to . . ."

"It's a chance for the Mayor to put me away for good."

"No, that's not true. He promised to . . ."

"Promises," sneered Hector. "Like he promised to help the people and then when he got elected he closed down the hospitals and the schools and the day-care centers, just like the bankers told him to."

Jillian shook her head and looked at Jack.

"This is different," said Jack. "All he promised was to listen to you."

"For a lousy five minutes."

"That's five minutes more than you ever had before." Jack struggled to keep his rising anger out of his voice.

"How come he wants me alone? And *inside* the park, where he's got me fenced in?"

"He wants the meeting to be secret," said Jillian. "You can understand that."

"Sure. So no one sees his pigs take me off."

"I've got an idea," said Jillian. "I'll stay here with your, uh, collective, until you're back from the meeting."

Hector's eyes narrowed. "You mean like a hostage?"

"That's right," said Jillian.

"No way," said Jack.

"This is my decision," said Jillian.

"Forget that," said Hector. "I don't need no phony kidnap rap, too. Give them an excuse to come up here shooting."

"You're paranoid," said Jillian.

"Paranoid is when you *think* they're out to get you," said Hector. "We *know*."

"Then maybe," said Jillian, "you're just afraid."

Jack heard the squeak of sneakers on the stone floor. He imagined the shadowy figures shifting from foot to foot. He wondered how many there were and if they were as hot and tired and angry as he was.

Hector laughed, a barking sound that echoed in the lobby. "Psy-chol-o-gy. You think every Latino is so

116

screwed up with machismo, all you got to do is press the button and he'll do what you want?"

"You've got to go all the way with this," said Jack. "You've got to finish what you start."

"That's pitching a baseball game, man, that's not life." Hector unfolded his arms. His hands were balled into fists. "You don't know nothing about people, what they got to do to survive."

"It's all the same. If you believe in something, once you start it, you've got to go the distance."

"Go the distance," mimicked Hector. "Man, you just a-maze me, come up here with your slogans, like you think this is some big locker room. This ain't no game up here, this is for real. Go play ball and leave us alone."

"Jack's got a game today," said Jillian. Her voice was rising. "In just a few hours. In Yankee Stadium. Do you think he'd come here if he didn't believe . . ."

"That true?" Hector came down the steps. "You playing in Yankee Stadium today?"

Jack nodded. "The Metro Area Championship."

"I didn't know that." His eyes bugged as the Mayor's had. He shouted something in Spanish and half a dozen bodies materialized from the shadows. "Wait here. I got to talk with my people."

Hector led the others out of the lobby. A door opened, then slammed shut on the muffled shouts of an argument.

Jillian plopped down on the marble steps. Jack sat down beside her. "It's funny," he said. "The Mayor and Hector, they both decide I'm sincere when they find out I've got a game today."

117

"They think you're risking a lot, doing all this right before you've got to pitch."

"It's just a game." Jack jerked a thumb toward the ceiling. "Compared to those little kids upstairs."

"I don't think too many jocks would do what you're doing."

"Sure they would. If they got to see this. Just because you spend a lot of time playing ball doesn't mean you're not a human being."

She rested her head on his shoulder. "I am so tired. You must be, too."

"A little."

She rummaged in a pocket of her jacket. "I've got something here. . . ." She fished out two little pill boxes, one silver, one gold. Jack recognized the silver box. She had taken a white capsule out of that box and swallowed it, when Grandma had given her a hard time on the deck. She flicked open the lids of the boxes with her thumbnails. "The white is a very mild trank to mellow you out and the green is a very mild amphetamine to get your rear in gear."

"We don't need them," he said.

She leaned away to get a better view of his face. "Hey, what's wrong?"

"I can't stand to see you stoned."

"I was up all night printing those pictures, I need . . ."

Jack stood up. "Do what you want."

". . . something to keep me going."

"Take the whole box, both boxes, Jillian, you should

have seen what you looked like that night, blank, zip, you could have been on Mars for all you knew." His voice bounced off the stone lobby walls.

"It was medication," she said weakly. "Prescribed medication."

"It made you a zombie."

"These are different. They're just little helpers. That's all they are."

"It's all the same, one thing leads to another, and I don't want any part of it." He couldn't help shouting.

"You're not being fair," she cried.

"I know that, and I'm sorry, but that's the way I feel." He had the sensation of watching himself as he shouted and gestured. Who is this guy? Not Cool Jack. But he felt good about saying what he was feeling.

"Wait a minute. Where do you come off putting a trip like this on me?" Her voice was strong again. "What about the shots for your elbow?"

"That's different."

"I don't think so," said Jillian.

"It's so I can pitch."

"I take drugs so I can function."

"There are people depending on me." Listening to himself, he wasn't so sure he was making sense. But he plunged on. "The team. Coach. My family."

A metal door banged open and Hector stomped into the lobby. "You got it. With two changes." He gestured at the sullen group behind him. "My people think it's a trap, but I'll take the chance."

"What changes?" asked Jillian.

119

"I ain't coming alone. There got to be witnesses in case it's a ambush."

"You think the Mayor's going to double-cross his friends' daughter?" asked Jack.

"Why not?" Hector laughed his sharp bark. "He double-crosses everybody else."

"What's the other change?" asked Jillian.

"The meeting got to be *outside* the park. Otherwise I'm like a rat in a trap."

"I don't think he'll go for that," said Jillian. "He wants a secret meeting."

"How about this," said Jack. "Meet him inside the park, but bring two of your people. No guns or knives, though."

Hector frowned. "You really trust this Mayor, Jack? You really think he's sincere?"

"I do," said Jack.

Hector stared at Jack for a long time before he said, "Okay. You know why I'm gonna do it your way, man? Because you the most straight dude I ever met in my life. If I can't trust you, Jack, I never trust nobody."

They shook hands. Jack looked down into Hector's black marble eyes. They seemed softer, friendlier than he had ever imagined they could be toward him. He felt a sudden warmth toward Hector. Maybe someday they'd get to know each other a little better. Go to a ball game together. Take him fishing at the reservoir. He thought of words to express his feeling: Hey, brother, if only one of us can win today, I hope it's you, Hector. But all he said was: "Good luck." He punched Hector lightly on the arm.

Jillian leaned forward suddenly and kissed Hector's cheek. "Next time we're here, I hope we'll all be painting and hammering and turning this place into a palace."

"That's the dream," said Hector. He shouted something in Spanish and put a hand on each of their arms. He guided them toward the front door. "The car be right here." At the door, he squeezed Jack's arm. "Pitch good, man. Anybody crowd the plate on you, stick it in his ear." He laughed and pushed them out into the hot, windy afternoon.

An old, rusted red Pinto was waiting for them outside the building. It was the same car that had taken them back to Yankee Stadium after their evening on the roof, and the same driver, a slim, silent young woman with dark, fierce features. Jillian smiled and said hello to her, but she only glared back. She said nothing on the brief, jerky ride. Twice, she made four right turns in a row to make sure they weren't being followed. Just like the private eyes on television, thought Jack. She let them off under the shadow of the elevated subway tracks alongside the Stadium.

From a distance, they heard the brain-rattling thunder of an approaching subway train.

"I better get going. I'll come back up with the Mayor in the limo, and make sure he understands about the change." She threw her arms around his neck. "Good luck. I'll be rooting for you."

"Aren't you going to the meeting?"

"You think I should?"

121

"Yeah. It's more important than the game. Come back when the meeting's over and tell me what happened."

"But you'll be pitching. Won't it spoil your concentration?"

"It'll be all right. Just come down to the rail, I can talk to you when we're at bat."

"If you're sure . . ."

"Positive." He kissed her.

Howling and clattering, the train began its long slide into the station.

He watched her run up the steps to the elevated platform. He waited until her train was storming downtown toward City Hall before he crossed the street to Yankee Stadium.

21

Coach Burg was pacing in front of the Stadium's main entrance, slamming his right fist into his left palm, glancing anxiously up and down the street. From a distance, he seemed smaller than Jack remembered him, and almost comical. His yellow-and-black Nearmont baseball cap rode high on his head, and his black nylon warm-up jacket billowed out behind him as he paced and spun and smacked his hands.

When he saw Jack, he threw up his arms and began waving as if he were signaling a base runner home. He shouted, "C'mon, big fella, let's go."

Without thinking, Jack broke into a trot. After a few steps, he pulled up short. There's plenty of time, he thought. I'm my own man, I don't jump for anyone.

But the sight of the coach's face, red and twisted with worry, started him running again.

"You okay?" When Jack nodded, Coach Burg's face sagged with relief. He grabbed Jack's arm and hustled him through the gate. "What's this business with the Mayor?"

"I had something important to do." He liked the way he said it, not apologetically, not cocky, just matter-of-fact.

"More important than this game?" They were hurrying through a dark, cool tunnel inside the Stadium.

"The game doesn't start till four," said Jack.

"Doc wanted to shoot the elbow at least three hours before game time, in case it needs a booster."

"A second shot?" Jack stopped. "But he hasn't even examined me, he doesn't know if . . ."

"I'm not taking any chances." The coach pulled him along.

"Where are my folks?"

"They're up the wall," said Coach Burg.

"I left them a note." Jack felt a pang of guilt.

"That's never enough. Someday you'll understand. Here we go." Coach Burg shouldered open an unmarked metal door and yanked Jack into a large, bright dressing room.

The Nearmont players were standing in front of open wooden cubicles, changing into their uniforms. Some cheered, a few clapped as the coach led Jack across the dressing room. Joey DiNola blew a welcome. Pete Reynolds let loose a rebel yell.

Dr. May looked up from taping an ankle, handed the tape roll to a student trainer and followed them into a small room, bare except for an empty desk and a wooden chair. Coach Burg released Jack and kicked the door shut. "Can you still do it, Doc?"

Dr. May checked his watch. "We've blown the medication sequence, but I think I can adjust the dosage. One big shot instead of two smaller ones."

"I thought you were going to examine the elbow first." Jack's tongue felt swollen in a dry mouth.

"If that elbow flares, you won't last an inning." Dr. May snapped open an attaché case filled with medical equipment. "Once that happens, it's Sorry, Charlie."

"Roll up your sleeve," said the coach.

"Wait a minute, I'd like to . . . ."

"I know where you're coming from, Jack." Dr. May forced a smile. His bald scalp was slick with sweat. "I can appreciate someone who cares about what goes into his body. Too many jocks'll take anything they think might give them an edge. But this"—he lifted out a rubber-stopped glass vial—"is medication to treat a specific condition. Your elbow inflammation."

"It's not inflamed yet, maybe it won't be. . . ."

"If it isn't now, it will be by the middle of the game," said Coach Burg. Little sweat blisters appeared on his forehead and under his eyes.

"How can you be so sure?" asked Jack.

The little room was hot, airless. Jack was taller than either man, but he felt like a child again, shrunken and pressed to the wall by their stares.

125

"I'm not sure," said the coach, "but this is too big a game to take a chance."

Jack blurted, "I want to talk to my folks."

"What is it, Jack?" asked the coach. "What's wrong? This isn't like you at all. Is it that girl?"

What can I say to him thought Jack. I promised my Grandma I would check with her first?

He took a deep breath. He wanted to tell the coach that none of them would be here today if it wasn't for his pitching this season, that they had no right to fill his elbow with chemicals that could bubble up in ten, twenty, thirty years to cripple or kill him, but the words stuck in his throat.

"Please. I want to talk to my folks."

Coach Burg's voice was soft. "They know about your shots. They know we'd never give you anything that . . ."

"I want to talk to them."

"I'll go with him," said Dr. May. "In case they have any questions."

"I want to go alone."

Coach Burg shook his head. "I'm not taking a chance on losing you again."

He opened the door and steered Jack out of the little room. Jack felt the team's puzzled glances as he and the coach retraced their path across the dressing room. Burg pulled him out into the tunnel and beckoned to an usher. "Can you get us up to our Booster Club? They're still on tour. It's an emergency." He handed the usher a few dollars.

"Follow me, fellas." He was a scrawny, white-haired man, but they had to lengthen their strides to keep up with him, down the tunnel, through a metal door, across a stone plaza, through glass doors, into a small elevator. Jack avoided looking at Coach Burg as the elevator zoomed up. He thought of a subway train. Jillian would be getting close to City Hall. Maybe she was already there.

"Just a little dose of the jitters," said Coach Burg. "Don't worry about it. All the great ones get it. Means you're on edge, ready."

"You listen to your coach," said the usher. "I been here thirty-eight years, I seen Joe D., Mickey Mantle, Reggie, believe me, the trouble with young ball players, they think they know everything and they don't know diddly-squat."

"Take a good look at this boy," said Coach Burg. "He just might be back here someday wearing Yankee pinstripes."

The elevator lurched to a stop. The usher led them across a concrete walkway, through a door marked NO ADMITTANCE and into a carpeted hallway. Jack felt numb, as if he was sleepwalking. Coach Burg's grip on his arm was firm.

Through the glass walls of the hallway, he could see into rooms that overlooked the playing field. The ground crew was preparing the diamond, whitening the foul lines and raking the infield dirt. One man, on his knees, was smoothing and shaping the pitcher's mound.

"He's getting that ready for you," said the coach.

127

The Tiger Boosters were crowded at the end of the hallway, looking through the glass wall at a young woman seated in front of a control board of buttons and switches and blinking lights. As her fingers tapped over the keyboard, words and pictures flashed on the electronic scoreboard in center field.

Jack scanned the backs of dozens of heads. He hoped he would spot Mom or Grandma first. They would understand more quickly than Dad how he felt about the shots.

The scoreboard exploded with skyrockets. From the middle of the crowd Jack heard Donnie's "Awwwww-riiiight." He began pushing toward him.

"It's Jack Ryder," said someone, and the crowd parted. Bucky Flynn's father said something to him and Joey DiNola's mother touched his sleeve but he didn't stop until he reached his family.

"Oh, you're here," said Mom, smiling.

"What's wrong?" asked Dad. "You're not dressed for the game."

Donnie hugged him. Over Donnie's shoulder, Jack exchanged glances with his grandmother. Her eyebrows were raised. He felt better.

"John?" Coach Burg pushed in. "Jack wants to talk to you."

"What is it, son?" Dad looked tense.

Jack waited until Mom and Grandma had pressed closer to hear. "It's about my . . ."

"Not here, Jack." Coach Burg was pulling him away

128

from Donnie. "You can't hold a meaningful discussion in this mob scene."

"Sure we can, I . . . ."

"John?" Coach Burg motioned toward a door with his head, and suddenly Dad had one arm and Burg the other and they were shepherding him through the crowd and back down the hallway and out a door. Jack felt helpless. What am I going to say, he thought. I want my Grandma? How would Dad feel about that? He and the coach might treat it as a joke. Or treat me like a child.

Out on the concrete runway, Coach Burg took off his cap and wiped his brow. The cap had left a deep mark across his forehead. "We'll keep this man-to-man. Better that way."

"What's up, George?" asked Dad.

"Suddenly Jack's uptight about side effects," said Coach Burg. "Like one more shot's going to kill him. Doc and I both think he should take it."

"So do I," said Dad.

He felt trapped between them. Coach Burg had maneuvered him away from the only person who might understand what was bothering him. He was on his own.

"Maybe my arm could hold out without the shot." He knew he didn't sound convincing. "Doc didn't even examine me."

"Doc says his elbow won't last an inning without medication," said Coach Burg. "But it's his decision, of course."

"It's a big game, Jackie," said Dad. His voice rose. "It's your biggest."

"They want to give me a new shot," said Jack, "something different. Cortisone and . . ."

"For God's sake, Jackie," shouted Dad, "if you can't trust George and Doc May, you can't . . ."

"Easy, John," said Coach Burg. "It's the boy's arm."

Jack looked at Burg in amazement. He sounded almost sympathetic. The snake. Let the pressure come from Dad. Jack felt his strength and control slipping away.

"What's wrong with you, Jack?" asked Dad. "One more shot and then you've got the whole summer to rest the arm. We can go to a specialist if you want. In New York."

"Make you feel better?" asked the coach. He was patting Jack's shoulder.

"You're lucky you've got a coach like George. A game like this, I wouldn't be so understanding," said Dad. "I'd be shaking you by the throat."

"It's a different time," said Coach Burg. "Ever hear of Jock Lib? Athletes have rights, too."

"Not to pull something like this at the last minute," said Dad. "It's like reneging on a promise."

Jack blurted, "What about his promise to help us? How is he going to help us with recruiters if he's at Harrison next year? He's trying to get a job there."

Dad cleared his throat. "Is that true, George?"

"Yes, it is." Coach Burg looked Dad in the eyes. "I didn't tell the boys because I was afraid it would put

130

too much pressure on them to win the game for me instead of for themselves."

Dad nodded. He's swallowing this whole, thought Jack. What can I say now?

Coach Burg said, "I'm sorry you found out like this, John."

"I understand." Dad brightened. "So when you come down to it, this is what was really bothering Jack."

"I'm glad we had a chance to get it out before the game," said Coach Burg.

"No," said Jack, "it's the . . ."

But the two men were already slapping his back and pushing him toward the elevator. Tension pain rippled across his shoulders and up his neck. The promise to Grandma seemed dim. One more shot. Big deal. He thought of Jillian. She probably popped pills all the way down to City Hall on the subway.

22

The arm was a whip, long and strong and loose. No pain. It didn't even feel as though it was connected to his body.

He reared back, kicked high and fired the rocket at the bull's-eye of Coach Burg's mitt. *Crack!* The good sound. The coach came up smiling as Jack recovered from his follow-through. "You got it, big fella." He pegged the ball back. "Couple more."

Jack felt a hot, liquid excitement begin to boil up from his toes and seep into his legs. Yankee Stadium. The Metro Championship. No team from New Jersey ever made it before. And I'm the starting pitcher.

Crack! The fastball pushed Coach Burg back a step. He laughed and waved the ball before he flipped it to Pete Reynolds to finish the warm-up.

Jack looked around. There were only a few hundred people in the Stadium, most of them family and friends of the players. A scattering of older men, the scouts and bird dogs. He spotted Mom and Dad and Donnie and Grandma in box seats behind third base, with the Nearmont Boosters. He didn't see Jillian or the Mayor. They'll probably come at the last minute.

He threw a curve and then a slider to Pete. Strikes. Not a whisper from the elbow. The medication was working.

The scoreboard trumpeted and flickered:

NEARMONT, NEW JERSEY

vs.

BAYWOOD, NEW YORK

for

THE METRO AREA H.S. TITLE

A burst of ragged cheering rose like curling smoke.

He smothered a nagging thought. What if the Mayor changes his mind about meeting Hector? Don't think about that now. Think ball. The only thing to think about now is winning this game, pitching well, for my family, for my team, for myself. If I do what I'm supposed to do, it'll all work out.

A member of the ground crew carried a stand-up microphone out to second base. A dozen men and women marched out behind them. Coach Burg and the Baywood coach walked out to join them. Ceremonies and speeches. How many had he daydreamed through? Jack stepped down into the dugout, took a long drink of water from the fountain and stretched out on the bench. His teammates made room for him.

He closed his eyes and folded his arms across his chest. Relax. Concentrate. Think about each pitch, the fastball, the curve, the slider, the change-up.

Break them down, one by one, each movement. With a man on first base. Second base. Third. Bases loaded.

Forget that. Not today. Not the way the arm feels today. No bases loaded today.

The public address system crackled. Words floated out like loosed balloons—"fine young men . . . spirit of America . . . lessons learned here . . . forever. . . ." They popped and disappeared in the moist, still air.

Concentrate, Jack. Think ball.

Backing up the catcher on the throw home from the outfield.

Covering first on the bunt.

"You get a chance to look over the scouting report?" Coach Burg was standing over him, smiling.

Jack sat up and stretched. "Not yet."

Across the field, the Baywood catcher handed the Mayor a baseball and back pedaled furiously to be in position to catch it. There was a flash of purple beside the Mayor. Jillian was leaning forward, shading her eyes with her hand. She must be looking for me, Jack thought. He started to rise.

Coach Burg pushed him down. "Save your energy."

The plate umpire yelled, "Play ball!" and Coach Burg moved to the top step of the dugout as the Nearmont leadoff hitter stepped into the batter's box.

When Jack looked again, the Mayor and Jillian were gone. To meet Hector. Think ball.

He pulled the typewritten sheet out of his pants pocket. It was already damp with his sweat. Beside the name of each Baywood player was the type of pitch he hit best and the pitch he most often struck out on or hit weakly. Coach Burg had personally scouted the team.

The names and the words wiggled and faded on the page. Jack's eyes were bleary from lack of sleep. He wondered if he should have taken a greenie. Coach Burg and Dr. May had conveniently stepped out of the dressing room just before Brian Mills started handing them out. Most of the guys had tried speed before, but it was the first time they had ever gotten it from a manager right before a game. They figured Coach and Doc knew about it, maybe had even supplied it, but didn't want to be involved.

Jack had thought of Jillian's little boxes when he picked two greenies out of the paper cup that Brian held out to him. Why not? He had already taken the shot. A couple of pills wouldn't make any difference. But he had dropped them back into the cup.

He shoved the scouting report back into his pocket. Don't need a pill or a piece of paper, not today. It's the arm that counts. Today, I can bring it. Those suckers will never see the ball.

Nearmont went down one, two, three in the top of the first inning.

"Go get 'em, Jumpin' Jack." Coach Burg whacked

his butt as he trotted out to the mound.

"Hey, Jack-eeeeeeeee."

He waved to Donnie. He thought of Kristie and their secret signal. The first time in two seasons she's missed one of my games. Seems like a lifetime ago, the last time I brushed the peak of my cap with the thumb of my glove for her.

But it was only last Friday.

Five days ago.

He threw two warm-ups and signaled Pete to peg it to second. Let's go to work. Joey DiNola started chattering as the ball whizzed around the infield. Dad and Donnie led the Boosters in a rising chant, "Jumpin' Jack *Ti*-ger, Strike 'im out. Jumpin' Jack *Ti*-ger, Strike 'im out." Even Todd Newman caught the mood. He pounded his monster claw of a first baseman's mitt and shouted encouragement.

The sky was smudged, inky thumbprints on blue cloth. Jack wondered if they were dark rain clouds or fires in the Bronx. Smoke rising from the charred ruins of another house where . . .

Forget it. Think ball.

The Baywood leadoff hitter stood very close to the plate. He looked like one of those scrappy little infielders who usually gets on base without using his bat, either drawing a walk or letting the ball hit him.

Okay, sucker. Ever see a sonic boom?

He blew three consecutive fastballs past old Scrappy, who stood there with his bat on his shoulder, his eyes popping out of his head. Who would stick his body in front of bullets like those?

Too bad Jillian isn't back yet, he thought. She's never seen me when I'm really cooking.

The second Baywood batter was a lefty. Jack watched him pretend to take a normal stance in the middle of the box, as if he planned to hit away. Don't try to trick me, sucker, not today. You're on the balls of your feet and your hands are too loose on the bat. When you get the pitch you want you're going to try to drag a bunt on Jumpin' Jack. You wish.

He kept his pitches high and hard and outside. Desperate to bunt, Lefty finally lunged for a pitch he should have let go by. He tapped it up in the air. Jack stepped off the mound and caught it in his outstretched glove. Two down.

Coach Burg was clapping and the Boosters were chanting and the infield was chattering. Ducks on the reservoir. Dirty jokes. The hot liquid excitement was rising in Jack's chest.

The third Baywood hitter was huge. A Wide-Body. He planted himself deep in the batter's box. No doubt about this one, he was set to blast a fastball into the seats. Fat chance.

Jack toyed with him, nipping the corners of the plate with curveballs that broke so sharply they seemed to be dropping off a table. Wide-Body nearly fell down swinging and missing.

The Nearmont team was yelling and laughing as they

ran back to the dugout for the top of the second inning. DiNola threw his glove at Jack and shouted, "You can *always* come late," and Bucky Flynn said, "I can hear it hum in center field," and Pete held up his reddened left palm. "I need an extra pad."

The Boosters started chanting, "We want a hit, we want a hit," as Todd, the cleanup hitter, led off the inning, and they screamed when he smashed a hit so deep into right field that even on his bad legs he got to second base without having to slide.

Jack borrowed binoculars from a manager and scanned the seats behind the Yankee dugout. No Jillian. Row by row he swept across all the first base box seats. The meeting between Hector and the Mayor must still be going on.

By the time Jack put down the binoculars, Todd was lumbering home with the first run of the game. The Tiger Boosters were dancing in the aisles.

Jack strode out to the mound for the bottom of the second inning with a two-run lead. Twice as much as I need, he thought. Nobody's going to touch me today. The hot liquid was up to his neck and his mind was a laser beam and his arm was a steel cable. I'll look for Jillian later.

The first batter went down swinging on three consecutive pitches.

He stepped into another dimension. The Stadium disappeared. The only sound was a steady roaring in his ears, the surf smashing against the rocks or maybe an endless subway train storming along an elevated platform to everywhere. The only other person in the universe was sixty feet six inches away, waving a stick at him. Puny little stick.

Dare you sucker even look at me like that. I'm Jumpin' Jack Tiger and I can bring it.

He knew the inning was over only because Pete whipped off his mask, leaped in the air with the third strike stuck in his mitt and trotted away from the plate back to the dugout.

He sat on the bench and heard voices. Faintly. Coach Burg said something, and he nodded, and Dr. May asked about his elbow, and he nodded, and Pete said something, and he nodded. Then DiNola jumped up and led the team out of the dugout and Jack grabbed his glove and followed them onto the field.

He could do nothing wrong. Fastball, slider, curveball, change. His mind rode the baseball, sat on the baseball and told it what to do from the instant it left his fingers to the instant it cracked into Pete's mitt. Baywood batters twisted and lunged and swung and missed. They held their bats at the end of the handle, they choked up, they tried to bunt. They stood with their bats on their shoulders taking every pitch, or they swung blindly. Didn't matter.

Twice, Coach Burg stuck a bat in his hand and pushed him toward the plate. He grounded out both times. So what. The lead had grown to five runs.

Far, far away, someone was yelling, "Jack. Jack." A flash of purple.

The hot liquid had reached the top of his head and

seeped into every muscle and organ of his body. He was an engine, a power plant. He reared back and kicked high and launched a beam of pure light. The batter swung from the heels and bounced it back. Two little hops. Jack picked it off on the rise and tossed it to first. The ball disappeared into Todd's claw.

Behind first base, at the rail near the Yankee dugout, Jillian was waving to him. Good. She'd made it back in time to see him smoke.

He held up the ball to her like a matador dedicating the bull. For you. He turned back to the plate. Wide-Body again. First two times at bat I fooled him with curves. He'll be looking for me to try to get him on another curveball.

"Jack. Jack."

Sidearm fastball. Just for you, Wide-Body. You'll never know what beat you.

Wide-Body started to swing, changed his mind and tried to stop. Too late. His bat collided with the ball and punched it to Matty Stein at second base. One bounce. Scoop and flip to first. Todd stomped on the bag and rolled the ball to the mound for the Baywood pitcher. Behind him, Jillian was waving frantically. Jack waved back. He couldn't make out what she was yelling.

When he got back to the dugout, Dr. May grabbed his arm and pushed the uniform sleeve above his elbow. "Pain?" Jack shook his head. Dr. May's fingers began probing and pinching.

"How is it?" Coach Burg hung on the dugout roof and leaned down.

"There's some swelling," said Dr. May.

"Can you give it another shot?"

He heard Jillian's voice, nearby now, but still muffled. He couldn't quite make out the words.

"I can't give him another shot, George, not after that big one."

"But we can't take a chance on the elbow flaring."

"Jack," shouted Jillian, "they arrested Hector."

He shouldered past Dr. May and started up the dugout steps. Coach Burg blocked him. "Relax."

"I've got to . . ."

"Two more innings, Jack, then you can do whatever you want." Coach Burg planted his feet and crossed his arms on his chest.

Jillian's voice was shrill. "They took him to jail."

He feinted left and when Coach Burg sidestepped to block him, he cut right and leaped the three dugout steps. Jillian was leaning over the rail alongside the dug out. Her face was streaked with tears.

"What happened?"

"We were walking into the park, and Hector was waiting there with two of his people, I even waved at Hector and he waved back, and suddenly somebody yelled, 'That's the one' and two men pulled out guns and started running towards Hector . . ."

"Who were they?"

"Police."

"Was it a trap?"

"I don't think so. But there were police everywhere, they caught Hector climbing over the fence and they handcuffed him behind his back and they threw him in the back of a squad car . . ."

"The Mayor just let them do that?"

"He went over to see what it was all about, and the police sergeant said that Hector fit the description of somebody who had just mugged an old lady, and one of his people, it was that girl who drove us, she said it was impossible, they'd been waiting in the park for a half hour, but the police didn't believe her and the Mayor said there was nothing he could do, it was a police matter."

"Jack." Coach Burg's hand was on his shoulder. "Get back to the dugout."

"They took him away?" asked Jack.

"The girl was crying, she said he'd rot in jail, nobody would help him, they didn't have any money for bail, it could be months before he even came up for trial. Oh, Jack, what should I do?"

"Leave the boy alone," shouted Coach Burg. "He might never have another chance at a perfect game."

Jack turned. "A perfect game?"

"Didn't you know?" asked Burg. "Seven innings, you haven't given up one hit, not one walk, nobody's gotten on base."

"Go finish your game," said Jillian. "There's time after the game to . . ."

"You hear her?" Burg was tugging on his arm. "Two more innings and you're in the record books."

"Hector trusted me." Something that felt as large and as hard as a baseball was rising in his throat. "That's

142

why he's in jail now. Because he trusted me."

"There's nothing you can do now," said Coach Burg. "After the game . . ."

"After the game nobody's going to listen to me. Now they will."

"What are you talking about?" asked the coach.

"That's the only time they think you're sincere," said Jack. "When you're risking your game. But I don't care about the game anyway, that's all it is, a game."

"Maybe it doesn't matter to you," said Coach Burg, "but it means a lot to your family and your friends and . . ."

"You got an eight-run lead," said Jack. "Kazuto or Josh can hold that for two innings."

"Two more innings," said Burg. Sweat sprayed off his face. Doc May and Todd and Joey DiNola were standing behind him. "Two more innings and you can do whatever you want."

"I'm doing what I want right now." He pushed away hands grabbing at him. He vaulted the fence. "C'mon, Jillian."

"Where?" She took his hand.

"We've got to tell everybody what happened, now, while we've got the chance, or else Hector'll just rot in jail and . . ."

"Jack!" screamed Coach Burg. "You're going to regret this the rest of your life. If you don't go the distance you'll never know if you're really a man."

"You're right," shouted Jack over his shoulder. "That's why I'm doing this."

23

He had never felt so strong and so free. Jillian matched him stride for stride up the concrete ramp. His metal spikes clattered on the stone and threw sparks. Her black hair streamed behind her.

He found the walkway that led to the door marked NO ADMITTANCE. He yanked it open.

There were more people now in the rooms off the carpeted hallway. Yankee officials in their offices. Sportswriters in the press box and technicians in the broadcast booth were getting ready for the regularly scheduled Yankee night game.

The woman at the scoreboard control panel looked up as he opened her door. "Sorry, no one's permitted . . ."

"You've got to put something on the scoreboard for us," said Jack.

"That's strictly against . . . ."

"It's life and death," said Jack.

"You'll have to leave." She reached for a red telephone receiver on the console.

Jack grabbed the back of her swivel chair and pulled it away from the console.

"What are you doing?" she yelled.

"Open that door," shouted Jack.

Jillian swung the door back and Jack rolled the woman in her chair out of the control room into the hallway. "I'm sorry," he said

"You're going to be very sorry," she shrieked.

Jillian slammed and locked the door behind her. "Now what?"

"We'll have to do it ourselves."

Below them, the Baywood team was jogging off the field. Bottom of the eighth.

"What about your game?" she asked.

"How could I keep on playing?"

"I shouldn't have told you, I should have waited. A perfect game."

"Nothing's perfect." He strode to the console.

"Can you really work that thing?" Her eyes sparkled. The most beautiful girl I've ever seen, he thought. "You are really something."

"It's like a computer keyboard." He activated the switches. "I took Basic Programming this semester, but

145

I missed a lot of classes for practice. I think I can figure this out if I can find the manual." He opened a drawer under the console.

There was a knock on the door. A muffled shout.

He found the manual and a set of index cards with the codes for programmed messages. A trumpet flourish was 14E. Attention Please was ATP.

The knocking had become a pounding. The muffled shouts were a chorus.

"Jack! Look!"

Faces were pressed to the glass wall of the room. Ushers, guards, the scoreboard operator, several men in ties and jackets, stood in the hallway and gestured to them. They banged on the glass.

"Ignore them," he said. "Concentrate." He tapped out 14E and ATP.

"How can we ignore . . ."

"Shut them out of your mind. Just think about what we have to do."

Trumpets blared. The scoreboard flickered and came to life. It read: ATTENTION PLEASE.

"You got it!" she shouted.

His heart was hammering. "Okay. What do we want to say?"

The red telephone began to ring.

Jillian said, "You remember what Hector said at the rally? About people dying a few blocks from here?"

"Okay. Give it to me slow."

He punched another trumpet flourish, then wiped the scoreboard clear.

146

"How can you watch a baseball game . . ."

He concentrated on hitting the letters evenly, in a rhythm. They leaped from his fingertips onto the scoreboard.

HOW CAN YOU WATCH
A BASEBALL GAME

The roaring was back in his ears and the hot liquid roiled and power surged down both arms. He felt as confident and powerful as he ever had on the pitcher's mound.

". . . while people are dying . . ."

WHILE PEOPLE ARE DYING

Down on the field, the Nearmont players were staring at the scoreboard. People in the stands were pointing. He noticed several Yankee players who had come early for their own game standing in foul territory looking out at the scoreboard.

". . . just a few blocks from here."

JUST A FEW BLOCKS FROM HERE

"I can't find the question mark," he said. "Does it matter?"

"They're trying to break the door down," said Jillian.

The control room door was shuddering under the impact of a steady, concerted battering.

"We don't have much time," he said.

He cleared the scoreboard and wrote:

IS HECTOR GUILTY OR INNOCENT

"Now they won't be able to sweep it under the rug," said Jillian. "It'll be in the newspapers tomorrow. On TV."

Metal screamed. Screws popped out of the hinges on the door.

ASK THE MAYOR

One of the hinges tore loose. The door began to tilt into the control room.

"Take over." He plunged across the room and hit the door with a shoulder block that slammed it into place.

"What should I write?"

He braced himself against the door. The battering began again. He felt the vibrations through his body. "Give those kids a chance. . . ."

GIVE THOSE KIDS A CHANCE

The second hinge tore loose. The metal door was thumping against him, faster, harder, thundering blows that almost knocked him off his feet. He tried to time the blows so he could brace for the impact, but they were coming too fast now, too hard. The door was loose and beginning to tip over.

Jillian threw her weight against the door. It slammed back into its frame. The two of them together might hold it back for another moment or two, he thought, but not much longer. He caught a glimpse of her face, proud, smiling, her wild, frizzy black hair tumbling over her purple shoulders.

"Whatever happens," she shouted, "thanks."

"For what?"

"I went the distance, too."

The door crashed down on them.

24

Mom, Grandma and Donnie were waiting for them on the deck. Mom got to Jack first and hugged him hard.

"That judge, what a baseball nut!" said Dad, trudging up the redwood steps. "We talked about the year Roger Maris hit . . ."

"Was that girl there?" asked Grandma.

Dad shook his head. "The judge saw her very early this morning so she and her family could catch a flight to California. They're going to check out colleges for her."

"That's justice for you," said Grandma. "The rich bitch gets off scot-free . . ."

"Jillian got the same sentence I did."

"Exactly?"

"Three months probation, we have to stay away from

each other, and if we don't get into any more trouble the charges will be wiped off the books. Didn't Dad tell you all that on the phone?"

"What about that Puerto Rican boy?" asked Grandma. "He got all that publicity, they're talking about a TV movie . . ."

"Hector didn't do anything wrong, Grandma. The police admitted it was a case of mistaken identity. You think the Mayor would invite him down to City Hall and promise to help him get the house if he really mugged somebody?"

"What did you get out of it?" asked Grandma. "Besides a lump on your head?"

"Maybe it was all for the best," said Dad. "It's good to get this kind of craziness out of your system early."

"How soon's dinner?" asked Jack. "Time for Donnie and me to start our jogging program?"

"Awwwww-riiiiiight."

"That would be very nice," said Mom. "But first call Kristie back."

"She called?" asked Jack.

"She's very concerned about you," said Mom. "It took a lot for her to call, after what you put her through."

"I'll call."

"Oh, and Coach Burg dropped this off." Mom handed him a cardboard box. "He said to tell you he isn't angry."

"Why should he be angry?" snapped Grandma. "He won the Metro Area Championship, got his picture in the paper."

"He isn't really cut out to be a college coach," said

Dad. "Better for him he didn't get the job."

Jack opened the box. The Metro Area Championship ring nestled in purple velvet. Her color. But it wasn't her kind of jewelry. He wondered if it was his kind anymore. He handed it back to his mother.

"I think we'll jog past Kristie's house," said Jack. "Stop in and say hello."

"That would be wonderful," said Mom.

Grandma arched an eyebrow, but said nothing.

"That's good," said Dad. "Just like it all never happened. Except you're going to be a better person for the experience. Am I right, Jackie?"

"Yeah," said Jack. Cool Jack. He hoped his face was expressionless. Leaving the Bronx County Courthouse after the hearing, he had struggled not to look as sad as he felt. The hot, damp streets choked with fumes, drivers cursing through the din of honking horns and screeching brakes, seemed so special. He would never forget what he had seen and done in the Bronx. Oh, Grandma, how can I ever begin to tell you what I got out of it?

"No more pressure," Dad was saying. "A nice, easy summer. I don't want you to even touch a baseball until August."

"Eric called, too," said Mom. "He wants you at work as soon as possible."

"See?" said Dad. "Everything's going to be just the way it was."

"Before the spit hit the pan," said Jack.

"What's that?" asked Grandma.

"Just one of Eric's dad's expressions," said Jack. Smooth Jack. Let them think it's all over. Otherwise they'll be nervous every time I answer the phone or get a letter, thinking it might be her. And someday it will be her. She won't be in California forever. And it's not that far away. I won't be in New Jersey forever. Jock and Jill aren't finished climbing hills. Jill and Jock.

"It's a cute expression," said Mom, chuckling.

"I like it," said Dad. "Everything's going to be just the way it was before the spit hit the pan."

"Sure," said Jack.